"What Are ...

"You look at me with blazing green eyes, you touch me like a hungry witch, you laugh with me like a child—and every time I come close to you, you shove me away and say no, because I won't let you have everything your own way.

"What do you think you're playing at? Do you think I'm one of your pets, that you can call all the shots and then throw me a treat in exchange for unquestioning obedience?"

"No!" Vicky said hotly.

Race's hand moved from her hair to stroke her face and neck. She shuddered and closed her eyes, instinctively giving herself up to his caresses. "How many men have you tamed that way, Vicky? How many have given in to those green eyes?"

Dear Reader:

Happy Valentine's Day!

It takes two to tango, and we've declared 1989 as the "Year of the Man" at Silhouette Desire. We're honoring that perfect partner, the magnificent male, the one without whom there would *be* no romance. January marks the beginning of a twelve-month extravaganza spotlighting one book each month as a tribute to the Silhouette Desire hero—our *Man of the Month*!

Created by your favorite authors, these men are utterly irresistible. Joan Hohl's Mr. February is every woman's idea of the perfect Valentine, and March, traditionally the month that "comes in like a lion, goes out like a lamb," brings a hero to match with Jennifer Greene's Mr. March.

Don't let these men get away!

Yours,

Isabel Swift
Senior Editor & Editorial Coordinator

LAURA LEONE
One Sultry Summer

Silhouette Desire

Published by Silhouette Books New York

America's Publisher of Contemporary Romance

SILHOUETTE BOOKS
300 East 42nd St., New York, N.Y. 10017

ISBN: 0-373-05478-5

First Silhouette Books printing February 1989

LAURA LEONE

grew up in the Midwest and has been on the move, traveling throughout the world, since she was nineteen. Back in the United States for the time being, Laura teaches French, Italian and English to adults and "drifts a lot." *One Sultry Summer* is Laura's first book.

For the old gang at Briarwood—
thanks for the memories

One

"Who on earth is Race Bennett?" demanded Vicky, her brows drawing together in a puzzled frown.

"Race Bennett," the lawyer responded, "is Henry Race's natural son."

"Natural?" Vicky repeated blankly.

"Illegitimate."

"Illegitimate?" Vicky's eyes widened and her jaw dropped. "Do you mean to tell me...?"

The lawyer nodded.

"So Hank had a bastard. Can you imagine that?" Vicky murmured in wonder. "He never told me."

The lawyer's gaze was positively arctic as it rested on Vicky's face.

"The term 'bastard,' while technically correct, is perhaps not entirely tactful, Miss Wood, given its defamatory—"

"Yes, yes, of course. What's going to happen now?"

"Well that depends on you and Mr. Bennett. While Henry Race's will leaves you in joint possession of the

property, there are no binding terms. Should either you or
Mr. Bennett wish to sell the other his or her half of the
property, this could be arranged. The capital, of course, is
a different matter."

"Capital?"

"A sum of money has also been jointly bequeathed to
you."

"Money?"

"Yes. Evidently it was intended to help you keep things
going until the property begins to bring in dividends."

"Wow! How does Hank's family feel about all this?"

The lawyer's look of disapproval answered her question.
Vicky returned his look blandly. He was a tidy, small man
with soft white hands. He dressed properly; he spoke properly; he probably even slept properly. And on a beautiful
day like this, when she was dying to burst out of this oppressively plush air-conditioned office to shake her hair free
and feel the breeze on her skin, he was evidently content to
stay closeted indoors and shuffle papers.

He was naming figures, and explaining inheritance laws,
taxation and her new legal responsibilities. She forced herself to concentrate.

"Of course, none of this can be considered definite until
I know your and Mr. Bennett's intentions." He raised his
brows inquisitively.

"Well, I'm staying at Oak Hill and carrying on the
boarding kennel as Hank and I had intended before he
died."

"I see. In that case, we'll wait to see what Mr. Bennett's
plans are."

"Have you contacted him?"

"Yes. At his request I sent him, several days ago, full details of the inheritance and its conditions. Presumably he
will be flying into the Washington area within the next few
days, and then we can all three meet together."

"Where is he now?"

"California, evidently."

"What does he do? What's he like?"

"Really, Miss Wood, I can't speculate about a man I've never met. He is apparently an architect. He seemed a reasonable kind of person. And he was obviously surprised to learn he'd been so generously remembered in Henry Race's will."

"Is that a fact?" Vicky murmured cynically. Hank had been extremely wealthy. Surely even an illegitimate son expected to inherit something. "Well, then, presumably you or I will hear from him before long. And then we can settle matters."

She rose to her full height of five feet eleven inches and took the lawyer's hand in a firm handshake, feeling a twinge of malicious satisfaction when she saw him wince slightly.

Out on the street, she pulled the clips out of her curly red hair and let it flow freely down her back. A soft breeze, tainted by the smell and noise of traffic, touched her face. It was too beautiful a day to waste in the city. As always, there was plenty of work to be done back at Oak Hill anyhow. She walked down the street decisively; time to go home. As she'd expected, it took her ten minutes to remember where she'd parked the bright yellow van—being in the city always disoriented her. But before long she was in her van, speeding over the Fourteenth Street bridge and on her way into Virginia.

Once she was out of Washington, the roads became more familiar and Vicky relaxed; she whizzed along while her mind wrestled with other thoughts.

So Hank, amid the rest of his chaotic personal life, had had an illegitimate son. If the man was a professional, then he had to be at least as old as Vicky's twenty-seven years, perhaps older—so it had all happened a long time ago.

"Ah, Hank, my friend, it was always such a tangle for you, wasn't it?" she said sadly.

Henry Race had been a complicated, unhappy and extremely successful man. During the last three years of his life he had also been a second father to Vicky. More than a second father—he had loved, accepted and supported her in a way her own father never had and never would.

Hank had believed his life had all gone flat somewhere along the way. He and his wife hadn't loved each other. He'd scarcely known his kids, having spent so little time with them during their childhood. He'd been proud of his achievements but felt strangled in the noose of high society, political circles and the public eye. He'd had affairs but had always gone back to his wife. When he'd learned his heart was giving out and the attacks had begun, he'd come up with a dozen schemes for a simpler, easier life—he'd dreamed of getting away from it all.

Through their friendship and through their business association, Vicky had grown to know Hank for what he was, both good and bad, weak and strong, and she had loved him as a daughter. She'd been devastated to learn of his sudden death by heart attack. She had cried for hours that night, openly and freely expressing her emotions, as was her habit despite her rigid upbringing.

So, in the midst of all that, she reflected, there had been another son, one Hank had never mentioned to her. Her curiosity was strong. She'd never met any of his family; he'd always assured her she wasn't missing much. Was Race Bennett different?

She pulled off the main highway and headed down the country roads, sweeping through the rolling green countryside of Virginia as it climbed toward the Blue Ridge Mountains. She turned on the radio, letting the guitars and fiddles lighten her mood.

The day had grown noticeably hot by the time Vicky reached Oak Hill. It was only late May, and already temperatures were climbing. It looked like a long, hot summer ahead in the humid green hills.

Oak Hill Pet Motel. The sign guided her down a road she would have known in the darkest night. From the moment she'd first seen it, she knew where it led: home. When Hank had first installed her here, Oak Hill had been nothing but a few broken-down buildings on fifty overgrown acres. They'd had a dream: to build the finest boarding kennel they could. That had been three years ago. Today, as she pulled into the long driveway, the kennel was standing, modern, shiny and newly opened. At least Hank had lived long enough for that.

She pulled up outside the kennel. From the front, it looked more like a country club than a kennel. It was tall, designed in a mock Southern-plantation style with a lemon-yellow overhanging porch supported by six pillars.

Vicky opened the front door and entered the cool lobby with its stone-tiled floors and brick walls. She walked over to the glass window that opened into the receptionist's office. She leaned her elbows on the counter and tapped on the glass.

Ginny Murphy, a small woman in her forties, jumped up and slid open the glass window.

"Well, what took you so long, girl? Is his wife gonna sue you for this place?" Ginny asked, leaning her elbows on the receptionist's side of the counter.

Vicky grimaced. "We didn't even discuss that. She's probably got her hands too full right now to worry about small fry like me."

"So . . . everything's all right, then?"

"Not exactly," Vicky admitted.

"What is it now?"

Vicky walked to the end of the lobby and went through the door to the office. Inside, she slumped into a chair opposite Ginny's and explained the terms of the will as best she understood them.

"No kidding! So Hank had a bastard!"

Vicky smiled wryly. It did sound a little tactless at that.

"But I don't get it, Vicky. I always thought Hank wanted you to have Oak Hill when he kicked it. Why'd he suddenly drag in this other son?"

"Who knows? Maybe he regretted not bringing the guy up as his own and wanted to make it up to him at the end of his life. Maybe he didn't have anything else the family wouldn't fight to keep—after all, we can still hope they'll let Oak Hill slip away unnoticed. As far as I know, this is the only property that Hank's wife didn't co-own with him, so

I guess it was the only thing he could easily leave to an illegitimate son and a surrogate daughter.... Who knows?'' Vicky tilted her head back tiredly and closed her eyes.

"So what about this kid, then?"

"I doubt that he's a kid, Ginny. The lawyer said he's an architect, so he must be a grown man."

"But what's he want?"

"I don't know. The lawyer doesn't know. I guess he's from California. Hopefully he won't want to be saddled with all the problems of a new business venture, particularly one he knows nothing about; with any luck, he'll agree to let me buy him out slowly and go back to where he came from. I'm just afraid of what will happen if he wants to take half the money with him."

"Do you think there's any chance he'll want to stay?"

"I hope not. The last thing I need right now is for some city boy to decide he wants to go back to nature and learn how to look after two hundred dogs. I have enough on my hands as it is."

"Is he coming here soon?"

"I don't know. The lawyer seems to think so. Keep your eyes open for someone with a good tan."

"Hmm, I sure will, honey."

"And try to remember that you're a married woman," Vicky chided her.

"Do I ever get a chance to forget it?" Ginny sighed melodramatically.

At that point the phone rang. Their conversation ended as Ginny turned her attention to taking summer reservations.

Vicky meandered through the kennel, checking everything with a proprietary air. She looked into the shop, not yet fully stocked, where they would sell pet paraphernalia. She checked out the lounge, where they had invited local animal-interest groups to hold their meetings. Ginny's enormous son was asleep on the couch.

"Hey." Vicky lightly kicked his dangling foot.

One blue eye peered out at her from a mop of blond hair.

"Aren't you supposed to be in school?"

"I'm giving it up for Lent," Brian mumbled.

"Lent's over."

"Man, don't you know how school stifles my potential?"

"It looks like you're stifling my couch. Does your mother know you're here?"

"Shh!"

"Brian, in this entire county, there must be some better place to play hookey."

"I am waiting," he said with injured virtue, "for you to give me the money to go buy new parts for that neurotic tractor of yours. Then I will fix the tractor. Then I will mow the lawn. Then, if there's breath left in my body—"

"You're wasted in kennel work, Brian. You belong in the theater. Something tragic and long-winded. How much money do you need?"

He cleaned out her wallet and raced out the door before she could finish. "Bring back a receipt!" she called after him.

Vicky checked over supplies in the storage room and made a few additions to the work schedule. Then she slipped out one of the back doors and headed down the footpath that led to her cottage. She'd go home, have lunch, change clothes and get some work done this afternoon. As she walked through the grove of oak trees between the kennel and her cottage, she breathed in the fragrant air, let the sunlight stroke her face, listened to the whispering leaves. Home, she thought. She had realized that three years ago when she'd seen the rolling, overgrown green land. It was the first real home she'd ever known. She'd put three years of her life into it, seen her dreams and plans form into something concrete. Nothing and no one would take it away from her. She and Hank had begun it together. He'd left it to her to carry on, and she'd fight to keep it in every way she knew how.

She heard an eager yelp, which chased away her thoughts. A medium-size black-and-white dog came bounding toward her.

"Rebel!" Vicky hugged her. "Where were you this morning?" With expert hands, Vicky absently combed the dog for ticks, twigs and tangles. "Hungry?" A pink tongue slobbered on Vicky's face. "Okay, come on, you."

They strolled together to the cottage while Vicky mulled over various decisions and problems. Should she buy a new tractor or keep repairing the old one? Should they invest in a new chemical sanitizer, which was twice as expensive as the one they used but reputedly three times as strong? Should she hire more staff for summer now, or wait and see?

Two days later Vicky was up to her elbows in dog food. She had decided not to hire more staff yet, so she and Ginny were doing most of the work until the college kids who worked for her became available full-time.

She was preparing meals for various dogs and cats. While she followed the instructions on several different charts, Nadine, the head groomer, kept up a running stream of conversation.

"So I explained to this woman that her dog would *never* look like the dog in the photo, because the dog in the photo was a French poodle, and what she seemed to have was a cross between a German shepherd and an Old English sheepdog," Nadine said.

"Uh-huh," Vicky grunted. "Have you ever heard of 'Pebbles and Beads'?" She peered more closely at the chart. "Oh! It must be 'Kibbles and Bits.' Whose writing is this? Oh, it's mine...."

"But you know how these society types are...."

"Not personally."

"So she *insisted* I give it a try, anyhow. Well, the dog's neurotic to begin with—which stands to reason, since she drives him around in a little two-seater sports car and, like, this dog is *huge*—"

"Chicken? These people want their dog to have chicken? I hope they brought their own. I don't charge them enough to— Ah! Here it is.'' She pulled a container of chicken out of the refrigerator.

"And anyhow," Nadine continued, "there's no way this monster of a dog is going to look like a Westminster-winning French poodle. Now, Vicky, you know I'm good—"

"You're the best, Nadine. That's why I hired you," Vicky said soothingly as she wrestled open a mammoth can of dog food.

"Vicky," Ginny said behind her.

"Hmm?" Vicky said absently.

"But of course this woman was pretty upset when she saw the result, because *obviously* it couldn't have been what she'd hoped for."

"Vicky," Ginny repeated.

"Something must be wrong here," Vicky said, frowning. "A cat that eats peaches? Who wrote this?"

"So the point, Vic," Nadine continued, "is that—although I had *warned* her—it was a seventy-five-dollar job and this woman refused to pay."

"What?" Vicky's head shot up, the charts in front of her forgotten for the moment, her fist clenching a dirty spoon.

"I knew you'd be upset," Nadine said.

"Vicky," Ginny repeated insistently.

"What?" Vicky snapped again. She turned to Ginny.

There was a man with her. He was tall and tanned. His hair was light brown, streaked with gold in the sunlight, wavy and shiny. His eyes were a smoky gray, openly amused at the moment. He didn't look a bit like Hank. But she knew, with a sinking certainty, exactly who he was.

"Race Bennett?" she croaked.

"Were you expecting me?" he asked with an absolutely straight face.

"Not just now."

"You must be Vicky Wood."

His eyes were still alight. She could tell he was trying very hard to be polite. Vicky felt uncomfortably aware of her scruffy appearance and even more uncomfortably aware of what an incompetent, unprofessional twit he must think her.

"Yes, I'm Vicky Wood. How do you do?" She stuck her hand out. He met it with his big, strong one. He winced, not because of the strength of her grip but because her hand was rather slimy. "Sorry," she mumbled. "It's cat food. You can wash your hands in the sink." He did.

"Have I come at a bad time?" he asked.

"No, no, not at all. Look, why don't you have a cup of coffee in the office with Ginny while I finish this. Then we can talk."

Ginny looked very pleased with this prospect and cheerfully took the man back to the front of the building with her. Nadine's eyes followed his broad shoulders and narrow hips with interest.

"Nadine?" Vicky said.

"Yes?"

"Go away. I have to think."

Alone, Vicky worked quickly and efficiently while her mind wandered to the man in the reception office. What an introduction, she thought. No doubt he would think her some witless country bumpkin he could take to the cleaners. Well, as her military father had always said, it never hurt to be underestimated by the enemy.

She quickly distributed the pans of dog and cat food, with a friendly pat on the head to anybody who wanted one. Then she rushed into the rest room to wash her hands and face and brush her hair. She knew she still didn't look particularly imposing, dressed in shorts and a T-shirt, but at least she was tidier.

Race Bennett and Ginny were chatting like old friends when Vicky entered the office. Fickle Ginny had obviously been completely taken in by a bit of beach-boy charm. It took Vicky five minutes to usher her out of the room; Ginny seemed torn between adopting Race and leaving her husband for him.

Vicky closed the door and sat down behind the desk, hoping this position would give her a measure of authority. She and Race sized each other up. His eyes moved over her with admiration and some curiosity as he took in her Amazon-woman appearance: the long legs, broad shoulders, ample curves, smooth muscles and wild red hair.

She tilted her head to the side and narrowed her green eyes a bit as she openly studied him. He seemed relaxed, leaning back in his chair, legs stretched out in front of him. His rugged body matched the strong features of his face. But something in his mouth and eyes, a touch of humor, a readiness to smile, softened the overall effect and made him seem more approachable.

He didn't seem to mind her staring. In fact, he seemed to enjoy their mutual moment of open curiosity. Finally Vicky spoke.

"Hank never told me he had another son."

"I'm not surprised. I wasn't really part of his life."

"You were a big enough part of it that he left half of this place to you."

He hesitated before speaking. "I think it was probably a sentimental gesture. He was given to them."

"Did you know him well?"

"No. Did you?"

"During the past three years, I did."

They looked at each other. His eyes seemed to absorb more than they gave away. There was speculation in them now. Was he wondering if she was a gold digger?

"We might as well get down to business," Vicky said. "Presumably you don't want to take over management of a boarding kennel. Do you want to be my silent partner, or do you want me to buy you out?"

"It's not quite that simple."

"What do you mean?"

"I've looked into the figures and accounts. And I've had a quick look around the property. Hank left enough capital to invest in this land only provided we don't split it up. Once we've paid taxes and legal fees, if I take half the money and split, you'll almost certainly go under. In that case you'd never buy me out. I'd be silent partner in a bankruptcy."

These were financial worries that had been playing on Vicky's mind for several days.

"Are you proposing to let me have all the money?" she asked cynically.

"That's one possibility," Race said.

"What's the other possibility you so obviously have in mind?" she asked suspiciously.

"I'm an architect. My partner and I see a lot of potential for five to ten luxury homes on this land."

"Don't be silly. No one's going to buy a luxury home right next to two hundred yapping dogs."

"Precisely."

A weighty silence filled the room as Vicky realized what he was proposing.

"You mean," she said at last, "that you want to close up the kennel, break up the property into lots and build here?"

"It's a possibility."

"But that's ridiculous! We've already built the kennel here. It's operational. To simply tear it down and start building something else would be throwing away three years of work, not to mention hundreds of thousands of dollars."

"Look, Vicky, I can guarantee that it would eventually pay big dividends. Can you say the same of this business? When the capital we've inherited runs out, what will happen if we haven't started turning a profit? Do you know how many promising businesses go under in the second year because of insufficient capital?"

"Then I'll mortgage it."

"Then you'd better hope you can pay that mortgage, or the bank will pull us both under."

"I am *not* closing down, and that's final!"

They glared at each other in charged silence. Race's eyes were narrowed, but he seemed otherwise in control. Vicky knew her cheeks were flushed, and her fists were clenched on the desk in front of her.

Race spoke levelly. "Whatever we do, it's got to be something we both agree on, because we're stuck in this together whether we like it or not. Unless, of course, you want to take all the land and give me all the money."

She gave him an evil look. "In that case I'd go under before you reached the head of the driveway, and you know it."

"Well, then?"

"What do you mean, 'well, then'?" she asked irritably. She jumped up and paced the room in agitation. "Do you expect me to say, 'Fine. Go ahead. Bulldoze the place.' Forget it, buster. If you do, it'll be with me inside it!"

"What reasonable alternative—"

"Reasonable! Can't you understand that this is my job, my work, my future? That this is what I do? I've spent three years working on this. I don't care about what kind of profits you can pull building *houses* out here! What am I supposed to do—sit around in my cottage for the next five years while you hammer and nail?"

"All right. Calm down," he ordered. Something in his tone forced an unaccustomed obedience from her. She sat down. "I'm not some kind of monster out to tear apart your kennel, Vicky. I'm only saying we have to sink or swim together. I know we'll stay afloat if we go my way. But you were here first, and, as you say, your kennel is already here. If you can prove to me that you can keep us afloat, we'll let matters stand as they are. I'll get out of your hair and be your silent partner. When you can afford it, maybe you can even buy me out."

She watched him broodingly. It was a reasonable offer. Even generous. And she had no choice. "What do I have to do to prove it to you?"

"Well, summer must be the busiest time of year for a business like this, with everybody going away on vacation and needing someplace to leave their pets, right?"

"Yes."

"Let's see if you can turn enough of a profit to keep us going through the months after summer."

"And where will you be?"

"Right here."

"Here?"

"Oh, yes." He smiled wickedly. "I'll be silent, Vicky, but not blind or deaf. I want to know exactly what's going on."

"Haven't you got a job or something to go back to?" she asked irritably.

"My partner can cover some of it. Some of it I can do from here. But my main job this summer is keeping an eye on what happens here. We've both got too much at stake to take it lightly, haven't we?"

"I don't have any choice, do I?"

"None. Partners?"

He extended a strong hand. She slid her pale hand into his darker one, noticing they both had work-roughened palms: people who worked hard for what they wanted and held on to it fiercely.

"Partners," she agreed.

Locked into their new agreement, they regarded each other with suspicion.

"So," Vicky said at last, "I've got one summer to prove to you that we can make it."

"Yes." He glanced at the humidity gathering on the window. "One sultry summer."

Two

——

"Does he bite?" Race asked breathlessly.

Vicky had to admire his guts. It took a lot of courage to remain calm with a two-hundred-pound dog standing on your chest, effectively pinning you to the ground and giving you a very good view of lots of big, sharp white teeth.

"Bite? Not exactly," she said laconically.

The dog put his big cold wet nose against Race's; a second later a long pink tongue washed the length of Race's stunned face with a single stroke. The dog barked happily and pawed Race.

"Vicky?" said Race uncertainly.

"Okay, okay." Really, she thought, it was very unkind of her to laugh and refuse to help an unsuspecting victim of the playful Saint Bernard's affection.

"Come on, Myron, off!" she said sternly, taking firm hold of his collar and yanking him off Race with all her might.

Race propped himself up on his elbows and regarded Myron warily.

"It seemed like such a silly way to die," he murmured. "Or perhaps the god of pet lovers is taking revenge on me?"

"I like that," Vicky said, laughing. She pulled up on Myron's collar and pressed a hand on his rump, forcibly encouraging him to sit down.

A small, wiry man of about sixty approached them in the main back hallway.

"Sorry, Vicky," he said in a gravelly voice. "He just dashed out on me. And I'm gettin' too old to chase through the whole kennel to catch him." He noticed Race picking himself off the floor. "Hope he didn't startle you, son."

"Startle me?" said Race dryly. "Now, why should suddenly finding a dog the size of a Cadillac sitting on my chest startle me?"

The old man let out a croaking chuckle as he put a slip rope around Myron's neck. Myron licked his hand and started gnawing good-naturedly on his foot.

"Race Bennett," Vicky said, "this is Joe Hanley. He's an obedience instructor."

Race and Joe shook hands. "Race will be staying at the manor house for a while."

"You must be kiddin'. That place hasn't been used for years. Must be fit for nothin' but skunks."

"Perhaps that's why Vicky suggested it to me," said Race with a teasing glance at her.

"I suggested it," she said crisply, "because you said you wanted to stay here. The only other two buildings on the place that have running water are my cottage—which you are not invited to stay in—and the kennel. Now, if you would like me to set you up in a suitable dog run...?"

"Never mind," he replied easily. "The skunks can make room for me."

"Why don't you stay in a hotel in town?" asked Joe as he tugged his foot out of Myron's mouth.

"Well, I may be staying for quite a long time."

"All the summer," interjected Vicky. "And the town's too far away to keep an eye on me, isn't it, *partner*?"

Joe looked up. "Partner? What's going on here? Myron, that's enough!"

"How many obedience lessons has Myron had?" asked Race uneasily.

Joe chuckled. "This is only his second ever. He's already fourteen months old. The family just couldn't cope with the wear and tear anymore, so they sent him out here to Vicky. I usually just come out a couple of nights a week to teach classes, but these folks asked me to give a special private crash course to Myron here."

"Will it help?"

"Oh, he'll learn, all right. He's got a good heart and he wants to please; he just can't seem to understand that he outweighs almost everyone and everything."

"I see your point. What happens—"

Vicky interrupted. "Excuse me, but I have a lot of work to do. Especially now that I've been given a deadline."

"Deadline?" asked Joe.

She glared at Race in sullen silence.

"You might as well tell him," Race said evenly. "Everyone will know the truth sooner or later, especially with me moving in. If you're determined to make me the villain in this piece, you might as well get started now."

He sounded so reasonable that Vicky felt contrite for her show of resentment. Consequently she made her explanation much more neutral than she had intended.

"Race has inherited Oak Hill jointly with me, Joe. We've agreed that if I can't prove by summer's end that the kennel will be a lucrative business, rather than go bankrupt I'll...close down and let him break the land up into lots and build private homes on it."

Joe let out a low whistle. "Sorry if I'm buttin' in—but why did Hank leave you half of Oak Hill, Race?"

Race's eyes met Vicky's for a moment before he spoke.

"I'm his son."

"You're...well, how about that? Well, then, I reckon he did right by you. It sure is a beautiful place, don't you think?"

"It certainly is, Joe," said Race.

"Well...if you'll excuse me, I've got to go give Myron his lesson now. You can see he surely needs it."

"Surely does," agreed Race.

The old man led Myron away. Vicky took Race through the side door that led to the footpath. Most of the way she walked ahead of him, rather than beside him; it effectively eliminated conversation. Although a slight breeze cooled the air, it was a humid day, hot for the end of May. Vicky knew the summer would be grueling. And the manor house, abandoned for years, had no fans or air conditioning. The thought rather pleased her. She stalked gracefully through the oak grove while her mind dwelled with malicious pleasure on the thought of Race being kept awake night after night all summer by physical discomfort, if not by a guilty conscience. As a Californian, he probably would find it hard to get used to the cloying humidity of a Virginia summer.

She turned to point out her cottage as they passed it and found his gaze following the sway of her hips with interest. His eyes met hers, then traveled up to admire her fiery hair; curling wisps of it had escaped her ponytail to frame her face. Their eyes met again. His frank admiration flattered rather than offended. She stood still until he took another step forward, then she jumped like a startled animal. She tried to freeze him with an icy look, but his gray eyes danced with enjoyment.

"That's my cottage," she said coldly.

"I know. I'm not invited."

"That's right."

"Who's this?" he asked as Rebel came trotting around the house to greet them. Rebel sniffed his feet, his legs and the hand he extended to her.

"That's Rebel. She's my dog."

"Your dog? I would think that the last thing you'd want to see after a day at work is another dog."

"That's funny. Now, *I* would think in most jobs the last thing a person would want to see at the end of the day would be more people."

"You prefer animals to people?"

"Usually. Animals are straightforward, sincere and unpretentious. A dog is the most loyal friend you can have."

At this point Rebel, fickle, feckless Rebel, rolled over on her back and gazed adoringly at Race. He scratched her stomach.

"Of course," Vicky added, "they are not necessarily discriminating in their tastes."

Race laughed and straightened up. "Shall we continue?"

They walked a little further and came to the river. Although it cut through only one corner of Oak Hill, it was wide and deep. Vicky loved swimming in it in hot weather. An old wooden footbridge spanned its narrowest point.

"It's old, but it's safe," she assured Race as she led him across it. Rebel tagged along, eager for a piece of the action. On the other side of the bridge the path continued, eventually leading up to the back of the manor house.

The house, Vicky explained as they approached it, dated back to the early nineteenth century. A section of it had been destroyed during the Civil War and had never been rebuilt. The rest had been altered, added to, damaged and remodeled steadily for a century thereafter. The result was a peculiar hodgepodge of styles and tastes.

"The house has stood empty for most of the time since Hank bought it about thirty-five years ago. In those days he thought about renovating it and making a country home here. But for some reason he changed his mind. He always kept the land as an investment, though."

"Shrewd investment," murmured Race. "This land's worth a fortune now."

"Before Hank died, he started thinking again about living here permanently, so he put in gas and electricity. Of course, it might not still be working."

"I suspect you're enjoying this, in your own malicious way," he remarked.

She wondered if he could read her mind, for she had been enjoying the prospect of seeing him camping out in the living room. She loftily ignored his comment. "There *is* running water, but I hate to think what it will be like. I was the last person to use it, and that was at least six months ago."

She led him around to the front of the house. Race took in the overgrown tree-lined driveway and the stone benches and dry fountain in the derelict garden.

"This was beautiful once," he said.

"Yes, I suppose it was."

"It was," he said with certainty.

An overhanging roof supported by six white pillars shaded the wide front porch.

"That's familiar," murmured Race.

"Yes. We chose the same design for the front of the kennel."

She showed him how to deal with the lock on the ancient front door, and they entered the house together. The interior was musty, stale, dusty and dark; it did indeed seem fit only for skunks. Vicky wouldn't have suggested the house to Race if she'd realized just how inhospitable it was. As they went through the house she threw open shutters and windows, letting light and fresh air pour in.

Vicky realized there was scarcely any furniture at all. Everything needed cleaning, repainting, remodeling, redecorating, repairing.

Race was carefully examining his surroundings, studying the walls and floors and ceiling with an absorbed frown.

"I'm sorry, Race. I didn't realize it was quite as bad as this—I'm not that mean."

"Let's see the upstairs."

The upstairs looked just as dreary to Vicky, even after she opened all the full-length windows and the French doors leading to the balcony that surrounded the house.

"What a mess," said Vicky.

"Are you kidding? This is fantastic! This is great! To think you and Hank just let this house sit here and rot all this time." He looked at her as if she had committed some unpardonable sacrilege.

"Fantastic?" she echoed incredulously. "It's a heap of rubbish!"

"Rubbish? Rubbish! Look at this," he insisted, dragging her toward the stairs. "Look at the sweep of that staircase. Look at the detailed carving in this banister. Do you know what kind of wood this is? It's walnut, solid walnut. Look at the hinges on these doors." He pointed to the fancy iron work. "You don't see that anymore. And how about this? Just feel that door. Solid as a rock!"

"Uh-huh," Vicky agreed, somewhat bewildered.

"Do you see what he did, the guy who built this place? High windows and doors all the way around the house to catch every possible breeze from any direction. Wide arches, instead of narrow doorways, so the air can circulate more freely. Plenty of light because of the windows, but you'll never be roasted by direct sunlight in summer because of the overhanging roof. High ceilings to help keep the rooms cooler. They would have had high beds to take advantage of the air currents."

"You like it here?" Vicky asked in disbelief. Perhaps he had hit his head when Myron had knocked him down.

"Look at this!" Race exclaimed, peeling back an old rug to look at the floor.

After ten minutes of being virtually ignored, except for being forced to admire more architectural wonders, Vicky slipped away and left Race to mumble ecstatically to himself about flowing space and structural soundness. She went back to work and didn't see him for the rest of the day.

He appeared at the kennel the next morning in patched blue jeans and a faded cotton shirt. Vicky eyed him with amusement.

"You've only been here twenty-four hours and already you're dressing like one of my staff," she said. "Could this mean you're planning to work for your keep?"

"I don't need to work for my keep; I own half this place, remember?" He grinned as she scowled. "And I plan to leave the job of looking after animals in your expert hands."

"Thank you."

"I'm not here to breathe down your neck, Vicky."

"You just don't trust me."

"Let's say I think you would withhold some of the truth if I went back to California and waited to hear from you." She had no answer to that. He leaned forward, his smoky gray eyes both gentle and determined. "I didn't come to crush your dreams, Vicky. But I have a few of my own. If yours don't work out, rather than going into bankruptcy with you, I'd like to take a shot at mine."

Her green gaze was locked with his. She could feel the force of his personality reaching out to her, warm, strong, fair. She didn't *want* to be drawn to him, she reminded herself. She lowered her eyes, rejecting his attempt to communicate.

Instead of persisting, he changed the subject and the atmosphere completely.

"In the meantime, I'm going to spend the summer fixing up that fabulous house. You won't know it when I'm finished, partner. You'll probably kick me out so you can live there yourself."

"No. When you finally get off my back and go back to where you belong, I can make extra money by renting it out to someone."

"Ah, but you'll have to send me half," he teased her.

She changed the subject. "What brings you here this morning?"

"I want to borrow paint brushes, saws, hammers, nails, ladders—"

"Any stuff like that you'll find in the garage. And while you're poking around in there, you might give Brian a hand with my tractor. It's been very temperamental lately."

"Anything to make you happy, partner."

She glared at him. He laughed.

"Anything else?" she asked ungraciously.

"Well, you haven't offered, but since we're co-owners now, I was hoping you'd show me around a bit and explain to me how this place works."

It was a reasonable request, she thought. She put aside the staff schedule she'd been working on when he came in and picked up her heavy ring of keys.

"All right, pay attention, because I have to do this all the time for customers, and I don't particularly feel like repeating myself for you," she said bluntly.

"Yes, ma'am," he said with exaggerated subservience, his eyes sparkling in his unnaturally grave face. Vicky pressed her lips together so as not to smile.

"Right, now," she began. "This is the center of the operation. Any animal that stays here is checked in through this office. We take down any relevant information about him—his diet, health record, name, age, a general description—and enter it into our computer. Then we assign him a run number and take him back to his run. We also print out lists every morning of who is supposed to be groomed that day, who gets special medications, who needs to be watched for health problems, who's going home, who gets fed what.... All that confusion yesterday—"

"Yes?" His eyes showed the memory.

"That was because when a new animal arrives we add him to that day's list by hand; he doesn't appear on the computer printout till the next day. And sometimes, in the heat of the moment, we don't write very clearly." She waited for him to needle her.

"Every system's got its problems."

"The computer also has a record of everything I spend—supplies, payroll, bills—and everything I take in. If you don't trust me, you can always check it yourself."

"I never meant to imply you were dishonest, Vicky, just protective."

She led him through the comfortable lobby, showed him the shop, the lounge, the rest rooms, the kitchen and the storage room, explaining things as they went.

In the back hall she very carefully outlined their thorough cleaning and sanitizing procedures. "Disease spreads very quickly, especially among a lot of animals in a relatively small area. We take a lot of precautions. Any pet that stays here has to have his shots up-to-date: hepatitis, distemper, parvo—"

"I had no idea dogs could come down with so many health problems."

"Oh, yes. And that's just scratching the surface. There's also mange, fleas, hip dysplasia, permanent retinal atrophy, tortion—"

"I get the picture."

"Sorry. I get carried away." She smiled.

"It's okay. I like your enthusiasm." His considering look warmed her. She turned away, determinedly brushing off the feeling.

She led him inside an indoor wing of fifty uninhabited dog runs. They walked down the aisle with twenty-five separate, sparkling clean runs on each side. She proudly explained the whole system to him: the series of pipes, faucets and drains that facilitated fast, thorough cleaning; the simple, comfortable interior of each run with its raised, cushioned bed; the sliding guillotine doors, which could be either left open in nice weather to give a dog free access to his private outdoor run or closed in foul weather to keep him warm and dry. She pointed out the heating and air-cooling systems, the piped-in music and the intercom system. The music abruptly changed to something loud, rebellious and distinctly punk.

"Ah, Brian just got here," Vicky murmured sardonically. "And he obviously doesn't know I'm here. I told him not to play that stuff; it makes them hyper. But he claims it stimulates their latent thought processes."

"Their?"

"The dogs." On the speakers overhead someone screamed something vicious about the queen of England. Vicky rolled her eyes.

Vicky took him to the grooming room next, where Nadine cheerfully demonstrated her professional skills to Race on an indignant Lhasa Apso.

Vicky leaned against the far wall, watching. Nadine laughed and chatted easily with him. In turn, Race asked reasonably intelligent questions and absorbed her answers with interest; Nadine was obviously as smitten as Ginny.

Race was an attractive man, Vicky admitted to herself. He had rugged good looks; he seemed strong and honest and good-humored. But there was something else. Some hint of wildness kept well hidden, of dangerous impulses held in check, of a sensuality he could release at will.

He turned and caught her look. He saw her interest in the split second before she lowered her eyes, and she knew he enjoyed it. Vicky clenched her jaw in embarrassment. Those sharp gray eyes saw too much.

"Shall we continue with our tour, Vicky?" he asked with excessive charm.

She shot him a look of annoyance and saw with irritation that it was exactly what he'd expected from her. Nadine looked at Vicky curiously as she sullenly led the way out of the room.

She took him into what the staff privately called the "Rodent Room," which was intended for hamsters, rabbits, birds, mice, fish, turtles and so on. There was a vicious chirping as she and Race entered. A gaily colored lovebird hopped around in its cage.

"That's Mrs. Periwinkle," Vicky explained. "Careful. She hates everyone and everything."

"Some lovebird," said Race, smiling.

"She used to be *Mr.* Periwinkle. Then one day she laid an egg and the Periwinkles realized their mistake."

"Does—uh—she come here often?"

"She sort of lives here at the moment. The Periwinkles are getting a divorce and neither of them wants to take responsibility for her, since cleaning her cage is about as much fun as swimming with a hungry shark. So they keep paying *me* to do it while they try to palm her off on some unsuspecting relative. I secretly suspect she was a major cause of their breakup."

"I can see how she'd create a certain amount of tension," Race said dryly as the bird hopped up and down, screeching fiercely at him.

"I'll show you her only trick," Vicky said. She took a piece of brightly colored paper from a nearby shelf and passed it into the cage. Mrs. Periwinkle took it in her sharp bill, yanking it roughly out of Vicky's hand. Then the little bird began shredding the paper and decorating herself with it, carefully arranging it to stick out from beneath her wings.

"Well, I'll be damned," Race said.

"More than probable you will be," agreed Vicky.

"I think you're starting to take after your bird, Vicky." He grinned.

Their tour ended in the cat room. Dozens of comfortable, carpeted, spacious crates stacked two high lined the walls. Vicky explained the extensive cleaning procedures.

"Sounds like a lot of hard work," commented Race.

"It is. But it's a great job for anyone who loves animals. Besides feeding and cleaning them, a big part of the job is just trying to make them feel happy while they're away from home. So we pet and play with them as much as possible. Of course, being the boss, I seem to spend a lot more time with paperwork and people than with pets," she admitted.

A Siamese started yowling. Race's eyes widened. "It sounds like it's being tortured."

"Ah, that's Sting."

"Sting?"

"Yes. He's just trying to get your attention." Vicky laughed.

The Siamese rubbed his face against Race's fingers as Race put his hand against the front of the crate.

"You can open it if you want to pet him," Vicky suggested.

Race's long tanned fingers fumbled with the catch on the crate door for a few moments. Finally, unable to unfasten it, he turned an amused look on Vicky. "Catproof locks are as frustrating as childproof bottles."

"Everyone has that problem. Here, this is how you do it."

Her long hands touched Race's and gently guided him until the door was unlatched a moment later. His hands were warm and strong, slightly rough in the way she had noticed before. She knew her own touch was firm and gentle from years of working with animals. She felt his gaze on her but didn't return his look.

Sting leaped out of the crate and clung to Vicky's neck. The wild yowling stopped while he rubbed his face against hers. She heard Race chuckle behind her.

"You're not allergic, are you?" she asked.

"No."

"Good," she said, and let the Siamese throw himself into Race's arms.

They were a sight, the two of them, as they met nose to nose, she mused. Two pairs of dark gray eyes regarded each other seriously.

"Yowl," said Sting.

"Hi," said Race.

"He likes you," said Vicky.

Race petted and scratched the purring cat for a few moments and then handed him back.

"I'll show you a good spot," she said, and rubbed Sting under one ear. "They love it there. You can make friends fast if you know their favorite places."

Race gently scratched under Sting's other ear. Sting tilted his head sideways and rolled his eyes back in feline ecstasy.

"You've got a good touch," Vicky said.

"Funny, I've been told that before—but under vastly different circumstances."

She fastened her gaze on his hand as he patted the soft, furry bundle in her arms. An inch or two more and he would caress her body with that firm, rhythmic stroke.

"I've shown you the whole kennel now," she said, trying to break the spell. "I'm sure you can find your way around the grounds without my help. There are maps and plans and deeds in the filing cabinets in the office if there's anything you want to know."

"I want to know how you came to be here," he said suddenly.

Her gaze shot up to his face. His hand stilled on the cat. His eyes bored into her, intent and seeking.

"It was all my idea," she said, confused at his sudden change of mood. He smoothly slid his hand that bare inch or two from the cat to her flesh. His smoky gaze shifted to watch his fingers slide up the smooth skin of her arm and over the thin shirt covering her shoulder to trace its collar before his hand dipped under her thick red hair to rub her neck. Vicky couldn't move, couldn't breathe, couldn't take her eyes off his closed and brooding expression.

"You're tense," he whispered, gently kneading the muscles at the back of her neck. A strange warmth flowed through Vicky. She felt as if he were unlocking something inside her with those gentle, seductive motions.

"What are you doing?" She had meant to sound authoritative, but her voice came out husky and breathless.

He didn't answer. His smoky gaze traveled up to the hollow at the base of her throat and then followed the firm line of her jaw and chin. His fingers ceased their teasing movement to follow the same path as his eyes. His touch was feather light, teasing, hypnotic. No one had ever touched Vicky like that. She felt something dangerous escaping within her.

"Stop it," she ordered without conviction.

"Are you sure?" he whispered. His face was so near hers that his warm breath stirred the curls at her temple. She felt he must hear her heart pounding.

"Yes," she hissed.

He stilled. "Okay," he said, and dropped his hand to his side.

Vicky looked up into his face. He must be at least six-two or six-three, she thought irrelevantly, since there were very few people in life she had to look up at. The sunlight pouring through the window highlighted his smooth strong jaw and cast gold streaks through his brown hair, giving him an unlikely halo. His gaze traveled over her face intently.

"And stop looming over me," she snapped.

A smile tugged the corner of Race's mouth as he moved away from her. Vicky turned to put Sting back into his crate. When he realized he was being left on his own, Sting started yowling fiercely, completely shattering the charged atmosphere. Vicky felt a bubble of hysterical laughter rise in her throat. She was grateful when Ginny poked her head through the doorway to glare at Sting.

"What a troublemaker. When is he going back home, Vicky?" Ginny asked.

"Soon, I hope," said Vicky, looking directly at Race.

Three days later Vicky was sitting in the lounge with an unhappy customer. She could deal with the most rambunctious or stubborn of animals, but she wasn't good at handling people.

"Since I brought him home yesterday all he's done is lie around and mope. He doesn't bark, or play, or run around—"

"I see."

"I'm afraid that staying here has somehow traumatized him," said the woman fretfully.

Vicky frowned. "I doubt that. More likely he's just worn out. He did very little *but* bark, play and run around during his two-week stay here. He's probably just taking advantage of the peace and quiet at home to sleep it off, so to speak."

The woman changed tactics. "But how could you let him exhaust himself so? Don't you keep an eye on them? I had heard you were more responsible than that, young woman."

Vicky bristled. "What do you expect me to do, clamp his jaws shut? He was having a good time—"

"I think what my partner is saying, ma'am," said Race's voice behind her, "is that this was a kind of holiday for your dog. You went away on vacation to get away from your normal routine. Maybe you stayed up late dancing, spent a lot of money, ate rich food—although your figure certainly doesn't show it," he added charmingly as he approached them.

Vicky turned to gape at him. She hadn't seen him since their tour of the kennel, and he was certainly the last person she had expected to rescue her from this dreadful woman.

"What my partner is saying, in her blunt way—" he shot a teasing glance at Vicky's stunned face "—is that this was also a kind of vacation for your dog. You could almost say that they actually come here to misbehave, bark and bounce too much, chew up old rugs and blankets, spill their water buckets and overturn their food bowls and just do all the messy, noisy, sloppy, doglike things they're not allowed to do the rest of the year. And Vicky here puts up with it and looks after them so that you don't have to."

"I never thought of it that way," said the woman, her eyes crinkling in response to Race's dazzling smile.

"And of course your dog— What's his name?"

"Knuckles."

"Ah, yes, Knuckles, I remember him now."

Vicky shot him an astonished glance and opened her mouth to speak. Race stepped on her foot and then shoved her over as he sat next to her on the love seat. As his hand found hers and squeezed it, he turned the full force of his charm on the now completely satisfied customer.

"Of course, you've got to expect Knuckles to be a little tired after his holiday, just as I'm sure you and your husband are a little tired."

"Naturally," agreed the woman.

"But I'll tell you what. If Knuckles isn't back to his old self in a few more days, you just take him in to his doctor—"

"Vet," Vicky murmured.

"—vet," Race continued smoothly, "and we'll pay the bill."

As if he were telepathic, Race squeezed Vicky's hand tightly before she could voice a protest to that.

"After all, if by some wild chance, Knuckles did get sick, here, we intend to take full responsibility for it."

"Oh, no, young man—"

"Call me Race."

"Race. I'm sure he's just a little tired, as you say. I don't want you to worry about it anymore."

"My pleasure, ma'am."

"I'll phone you in a day or two just to let you know he's fine."

"That would be greatly appreciated. In the meantime, can I ask when you're planning to go away again?" he asked.

"Well, July Fourth, I think."

"Can I suggest you make your reservations with our receptionist, Ginny, on your way out, then? We're already filling up very fast for the Fourth, and we want to give top priority to good customers like you."

"Oh, of course."

"You might also want to mention that to any friends who are going away this summer, so they can be sure to book with us before we sell out."

"Yes, yes, I certainly will."

"Thank you for stopping by," said Race, standing up.

"Not at all. It's been a pleasure."

They shook hands, both ignoring Vicky, who sat dumbfounded in the love seat.

After the woman had left the room, Race plopped back down on the seat. He stretched out his long legs and grinned at Vicky with frank amusement.

"Is that what you call customer relations?" he teased her.

"I told you I do better with animals than with people."

"It just takes a little tact, Vicky. Instead of an angry woman bad-mouthing you all over Fairfax County, you have a satisfied customer coming back soon and telling all her friends to do the same."

"All right. I'm impressed," she admitted grudgingly.

"And it has nothing to do with lying. It was the truth, wasn't it?"

"Well . . . yes, but how did you know?"

"I said exactly the same thing you said to her. Only I phrased it in a way she could appreciate."

"Hmm . . ." Vicky mulled it over for a moment.

"When I came in I thought you were going to bite her."

A smile played at the corners of her mouth as she caught his eye. The memory of him turning the conversation around completely in her favor suddenly appealed to her sense of humor. She saw the answering gleam of laughter in the depths of his eyes. Her lips twitched. Then the next thing she knew she and Race were leaning against each other, laughing freely and happily.

Finally their mirth died down. Vicky relaxed companionably next to him, her body touching his. His hand rested casually on her thigh. After a few moments she felt him move it to gently, almost absently, trace the fine bones of her hand. She enjoyed a small moment of contentment, willing herself not to examine it too closely.

"What brings you here today?" she asked.

"I finally figured out what's wrong with your tractor, but I'm not taking money out of my own pocket to fix it."

"I'll get you some petty cash from the office. How much do you need?"

He told her. Her eyes widened in dismay. "That much?"

"'Fraid so, Vicky."

"Do you think it's worth it?"

"Can you afford to buy a new one?"

"Can I afford to keep sinking money into this one?"

He hesitated. "Normally I'd advise you to buy a new one. Seeing as you're under a strict budget—"

"Thanks to you."

"Thanks to Hank, you mean. He *could* have left you everything. But instead he tied me up into the bargain."

"And you immediately put me under pressure with threats and ultimatums," she reminded him.

"I can see we've already exceeded your daily dose of rational behavior."

She tried to yank her hand out of his, but he held her fast. He closed his eyes, and she saw the muscles of his jaw work as he tried to regain his patience. In the heat of the moment Vicky pressed her advantage without thinking.

"Why can't you just go back to California? You obviously weren't much of a son to Hank. He wouldn't have needed me so much if you had been!"

His eyes shot open. "Don't—"

"Don't you feel the tiniest bit ashamed of yourself? Neglecting him when he needed you and now coming back to claim an inheritance?"

He seized her roughly by the shoulders. "What do you know about it?"

"I know that Hank brought me here, we dreamed of building this place, I poured three years of my life into it, this is *my* home, and now *you* turn up out of the blue threatening to take it away from me!" She shoved roughly at his broad chest.

"And who are *you*? A beautiful younger woman who convinced a dying man to sink hundreds of thousands of dollars into *your* ambitions because you didn't have a cent of your own?"

"No! No, no...." Her jaw dropped; her eyes grew wide with distress. She had never thought of it that way. But looking into his angry eyes, she suddenly realized that in some humiliating and unacceptable way, those were the facts. "No," she said weakly, without conviction now.

Suddenly the hands that had been gripping her so fiercely pushed her away. He stood up with a barely uncaged violence. Those dangerous impulses she had sensed in him before were running through him freely now. He looked powerful and vivid. When he spoke his voice was low and charged with dark, conflicting emotions.

"I didn't want anything from him after he died. I didn't ask to be remembered in his damned will. I told you it was a sentimental gesture."

Vicky looked at him in bewilderment.

"Dammit, use your head, Vicky. Haven't you ever wondered why he didn't just leave me money or stocks?"

She shook her head helplessly.

"I was born in your cottage," he said flatly.

Vicky was still staring at the space he'd been standing in when he stalked out of the room. She heard the door slam behind him as he left the front of the building, followed by the angry roar of his car as he drove off.

She put her head in her hands.

Her mind was a churning whirlpool of sporadic, confused thoughts and conflicting, chaotic emotions.

He had been born in her cottage. It was his home after all, not hers.

She wanted to feel his touch again.

Was she really no more than a penniless young women who had convinced a wealthy old man to spend money on her?

He was Hank's son. He was her unwilling partner. He was a stranger.

He had called her beautiful....

"Oh, Hank," she groaned miserably. "What the hell were you thinking of when you brought us here?"

Three

Vicky dived naked into the cold river, her long, strong body slicing through it smoothly as she swam underwater for several yards. She rose to the surface and flopped onto her back, taking in a deep breath of the sweet, heavy June air. She opened her eyes and looked at the bright blue sky filled with fat, fluffy, white clouds. It would be a beautiful day. And another scorcher.

It was the middle of the week, and a fairly quiet day at the kennel. Now that her college kids were working full-time, Vicky was able to enjoy a morning off work. The kennel had had a very busy weekend, and reservations for the following weeks were swiftly increasing. She felt highly optimistic.

The days were growing hot and steamy, and she came down to swim in her favorite part of the river nearly every day. It was only eight o'clock in the morning, and already the day was thick with humidity and the sun beat down on Vicky's pale skin.

She kicked abruptly, dived under the surface and came back up again to swim freestyle, her strong, smooth strokes taking her easily through the water against the current.

Vicky loved swimming, loved the water; she especially loved swimming in the moving current, under the open sky, with the fresh breeze and the cool water alternately stroking her bare skin. She was for the most part a physical person drawn to tactile sensation. She enjoyed physical work, physical contact, physical sports; she loved to feel, touch and hold shapes and textures that appealed to her, to smell, to taste, to touch. This was perhaps what gave her such a strong rapport with animals, since they were also tactile creatures. She usually preferred dogs to cats, since they, most of all, liked physical games and physical affection. Perhaps it was the result of her having grown up in a family so devoid of physical warmth. Perhaps it was simply the way she'd been born. And now, feeling the current caress her naked body and the hot sun stroke her skin, she gave herself over to a feeling of contentment.

After a few minutes thoughts of Race came creeping back to disturb her. She hadn't spoken to him alone for over a week. In fact, since their disturbing conversation that day at the kennel, she'd scarcely even seen him, and only once spoken at length with him when she'd asked him to go with Brian to buy a new tractor. It had arrived yesterday, and Brian looked as proud as a new husband; they were still maintaining the old tractor as a backup.

Vicky smoothly turned over on her back. Her red hair spread about her head like a dark fan as she floated lazily.

So Race had been born at Oak Hill. It explained why Hank had left half of it to him. She felt contrite and ashamed of her recent resentful behavior toward Race. If he'd spent his boyhood here, perhaps his tie to the land was as strong as hers. If he was Hank's son, perhaps he had more of a right to it than she did. Perhaps he had always understood Hank would leave Oak Hill to him; then he'd arrived to find a redheaded virago snarling at him to get off her property.

In all fairness, what did she know about Race? Nothing. And what did she really know about Hank's past? Almost nothing.

Funny, she'd thought she'd known Hank so well, but now she was realizing how little she had ever known. Only what he'd told her. And that had been sketchy and selective. She really knew nothing about how he had come by Oak Hill, why he had let it go to ruins or who had been his mistress and borne him a son here more than thirty years ago.

And what did Race know about her? Well, he'd certainly made that clear. Vicky was headstrong and emotional, but she never flinched when presented with the truth. He had phrased it in an ugly way, but he had spoken the truth. She had been toying with a private ambition to someday build a place of her own. She knew Hank personally, knew of his interest in animals and his generous contributions to animal welfare societies. When she'd found out about the derelict land so close to the Washington area, she'd outlined her ideas to him. She'd swept him along on the tide of her enthusiasm until one day they'd formed a partnership; he had provided the land and the money; she'd planned and executed every detail, from the initial site selection all the way down to choosing their letterhead. Yes, she had convinced a wealthy, disillusioned old man to invest in her ambitions.

But "a beautiful younger woman"? Did Race really picture her as some kind of vamp, luring Hank with the promise of her luscious young body? Vicky laughed out loud. No, that was absurd. For one thing, in all the time she'd known Hank, he had never behaved in anything but a fatherly way toward her. And anyhow she was hardly the femme fatale type; more like a Viking woman.

Vicky somersaulted gracefully in the water and did a lazy backstroke with her eyes closed.

For most of her life she had been a tall, skinny, big-boned, freckle-faced girl with frizzy red hair; gawky, gangly, shy and totally unattractive to her shorter male peer group. Then, when she was seventeen, a startling thing happened. She'd suddenly "filled out" and become plump in all the places a girl was supposed to be plump while remaining trim in all the places a girl was supposed to be trim. She'd grown her red hair long so the weight of it removed most of the frizz. Even some of her freckles had faded.

Suddenly boys her age had followed her everywhere, asked her out, tried to buy her root beers and pizzas. The sudden attention and approbation of people who would have ignored her as plain and dull only a year before had merely increased Vicky's certainty that most people were shallow, inconstant and insincere. What did beauty matter in the face of kindness, strength, fairness, humor, honesty?

A girl at college had once ingenuously remarked that with a body like that Vicky could get any man alive. Vicky had smiled wryly. Most men were far too egotistical to date a woman as tall as or taller than they were. Others believed a woman built like Vicky didn't have a brain in her head or an idea of her own. She had soon disillusioned that type.... With most men, as with most people in general, she simply never felt comfortable and couldn't talk freely, even if they seemed nice and genuinely interested in her.

Anyway, there was too much work these days to spare time for a love life. And if she changed her mind, there was always that veterinarian, Dean Alexander, who'd been coming by the kennel rather often lately....

"Daydreaming?"

The question startled Vicky so much her head went underwater and she came up choking, flailing and sputtering—hardly an attractive sight first thing in the morning, she thought ruefully. It was Race, of course. Who else would creep up on cat's feet and nearly drown her with a simple question? she wondered irritably as she trod water. She shook the water out of her eyes and glared at him. He was perched comfortably on a rock, dressed in old khaki clothes. The sun glinted on his hair, and sitting against the blue sky and above the glimmering water with his legs dangling carelessly and a naughty grin on his face, he looked for all the world like a mischievous guardian angel come to torment her.

"Been sitting there long?" she asked suspiciously.

"A little while. You looked so peaceful I didn't want to disturb you. Like a water nymph taking her ease in our river," he said wickedly. "Then I thought I ought to keep you from drowning in your sleep. It does happen, you know."

"Thanks," she said sourly.

"Don't mention it."

"Were you looking for me?" she asked.

"Yup."

"Why?"

"To see if we could call a cease-fire."

"It's been more of a cold war."

"Touché," he said appreciatively. "I need a small favor."

"I might have known." Vicky moved to float on her back, then thought better of it. "What do you want?"

"I'm installing overhead fans in the house, but in the meantime I was hoping you had a spare electric fan you could lend me. It's hottin' up somethin' fierce over there," he said in a fair imitation of the local accent.

"A fan?" she repeated doubtfully,

"I know you've been cherishing the image of me sleeplessly sweating away unbearably hot nights over there—" Vicky shot straight up in the water and looked at him with wide eyes. He grinned knowingly. "—but I'm appealing to your humanitarian instincts."

Vicky had to laugh, caught red-handed in a sense. "Okay. There's an extra one in the office at the kennel you can have for a while. I'll get it for you...if you'll turn your back like a gentleman for a moment."

"Is that part of the deal?" he asked.

"'Fraid so."

With a theatrical sigh he turned and stared at the grass with exaggerated attention.

Vicky climbed out of the river, squeezed the water out of her hair and reached for her towel before Race could forget his manners. Once she was properly wrapped in terry cloth, as if alerted by some sixth sense, Race turned back around instantly and asked innocently, "Can I dry you?"

"One favor a day is all you get," she scolded him. "How'd you know where to find me?"

"I've seen you down here before. Great view of this spot from the upstairs window. Took a lot of self-discipline to remind myself that we weren't on speaking terms, let alone skinny-dipping terms."

"I don't skinny-dip," said Vicky with dignity. "I swim in the nude. I'm sure there's got to be a difference. Skinny-dipping sounds so...adolescent."

"My mistake. And to be honest, swimming in the nude does sound more exciting."

"Actually, I'm glad you came by," she admitted.

"You are?"

"Uh-huh." Vicky pulled a knee-length T-shirt over her head and let the towel slip to the ground. She picked it up and started drying her hair. She sat down in a sunny patch of grass while Race watched her. Finally she stopped and looked up at him with wide, candid eyes as green as Oak Hill's grass.

"I guess I feel like I should say I'm sorry," she said.

"That's a pretty qualified apology." He was amused.

"All right, I'm sorry."

He came to sit on the grass beside her. "What for?"

"Well—for everything: For behaving like a sullen, spoiled brat. For trying to make you leave. For saying you weren't a good son to Hank."

"Why this big change of heart? Just because you know I was born here?"

"No. Yes. Partly."

"Ah, a woman's answer."

"Stop it. I mean, everything you said made a difference. About you. About me. I guess—I guess I wasn't willing to see it quite that way, but I have to admit that what you said about me is true."

He'd been gazing at the water. Now he turned quickly to look at her. He was obviously surprised. Then his gray eyes narrowed and he said coldly, "I see."

Vicky shifted uncomfortably. "And if you were a boy here, then I can see that from your point of view *I'm* the one who doesn't belong—"

"I never said—"

"—so I won't keep trying to talk you into leaving. I'll stick to our bargain fair and square. And if I lose, I'll give in without a fight."

A slight smile tugged the corner of Race's firm mouth. He said, "From what I've seen of you so far, I find that hard to imagine."

"Well," she admitted, "I might kick and scream a bit, but I'll come around in the end."

"Fair enough. I've told you before, Vicky, I didn't come here to ruin things for you. I just see a dream here for me, too, if things don't work out for you."

"Buildings?" she said doubtfully.

"Buildings." He eased his broad shoulders back onto the grass and turned his face up to the sun.

Unwilling partners, uneasy enemies, they enjoyed an easy and companionable silence, side by side on the grassy riverbank.

"I'd forgotten how hot it could get here," Race murmured after a while.

"How old were you when you left?"

"Ten."

"You lived in my house all that time?"

"Mm-hmm. Has it changed much on the inside?"

"I don't know about the intervening twenty years, but when I first got here there wasn't much to do, so I did a lot of work on it. Ginny's sons helped me."

"Hank really let this place go to the dogs after we left here."

She ignored his pun to ask, "We?"

"Me and my mom." For once his tone didn't invite conversation.

Vicky shifted and waited for him to continue, but the silence lengthened into minutes. Finally she prodded him hesitantly. "Race... won't you tell me?"

"Let sleeping dogs lie, Vicky," he said with a slight smile.

"Please, Race. I want to know."

He stirred restlessly and sat up beside her in the grass. "It's a long dull story and it was over years ago."

"It's not even over now," she insisted.

He seemed about to refuse, but something in her eyes must have reached out to him, for he acquiesced.

"Hank's wife's family used to own this place. When Hank and his wife Eleanore were first engaged, he bought it off her old man, figuring to fix up the gardens and refurnish the house to turn it into a country home by the time they got married a few years later."

"Hank never told me Eleanore's family once owned it, too," Vicky said in surprise.

"They owned it for years. Since the Civil War, I think. But they didn't use it much. They had other land in more fashionable areas; Eleanore's father was probably glad to let Hank have it. And it's one of the few things in Hank's name only, since he bought it before their marriage."

"What happened?"

"In the end they never used it, either. My grandfather and my mother lived in your house in those days. My grandfather was the caretaker. I remember the gardens at the manor house used to be beautiful when I was a kid."

"And your mother?"

"She was eighteen. She always insisted that Hank never seduced her, that she knew what she was doing. She loved him. Anyhow, when they found out I was on the way, he made noises about marrying her, but months went by and her pregnancy became more noticeable and he still didn't marry her. After I was born, she confronted him."

"And he had no intention of marrying her?"

"No. But it wasn't quite like that, either, though, to be fair to him. I think he wanted to. But he also wanted to marry into society and money. Eleanore's old man had already given him a lot of help, boosted his career, put him in contact with important people. He figured they'd wipe up the sidewalk with him if he walked out on her to marry a farm girl."

"Courage," Vicky mumbled.

"What?"

"I just remembered thinking that he was always so unhappy because he never had the courage to do what he really wanted to do."

"You'll forgive me if I'm not quite as sorry for him as you are."

"So what happened then?"

"Not much really. He never fixed up the house, never brought Eleanore to live here. After they'd been married a few years she found out the truth about me and never came near the place again. Hank paid to put my mom through college, paid my grandfather a good salary, paid for my education, sent me big birthday and Christmas presents. I saw him about once a year...." He paused, remembering.

"My grandfather died when I was ten. My mom decided to get out of here for good and start all over somewhere else. So we went to Chicago. That's where I fell in love with architecture, by the way. She was working for a big national company by then and got transferred quite a lot: Dallas, Denver, Philadelphia. Finally California. We decided to stay there when she met my stepfather."

"You have a stepfather?"

"Yeah, Wade. He's a great guy. In fact, he's my partner."

"Your what?"

"My *other* partner," Race amended with a grin. "He was a landscaper. I decided to go independent four years ago and talked him into joining me."

"Gosh. And your mother? Does she ever...talk about Hank?"

"She died six years ago," he said gently.

"Oh, God." Vicky held her head in her hands and tried to take it all in. Race, confident, charming, bold Race, denied a father and robbed of a mother. She felt him reach out to stroke her hair as if she were the one with the tragic story. Vicky rubbed her cheek against his warm, strong hand like a kitten seeking comfort. They sat quietly like that for some time. Then she raised her head and looked at him. He was the same man, full of quiet strength and easy humor, with no trace of bitterness or regret. Although he had a sad story and Vicky felt a warm sympathy, nothing about him could ever inspire pity.

"And what about Hank?" she asked softly.

"I've seen him only twice since we left Virginia. Once when I was a hotheaded nineteen-year-old and told him where to get off. The last time was about three years ago. I didn't hate him anymore, but I couldn't think of him as my father. He was a virtual stranger. I remember he looked so sad. And he'd aged...."

"Three years ago," Vicky murmured. Then, more abruptly, she asked, "Three years ago? Don't tell me he wanted you to design the kennel."

Race nodded.

"You refused?"

"Nicely, but firmly. He didn't know anything about my work. He didn't want me for my ideas or talent; he just asked me because I was his errant son and he knew he was dying. But it was too late to bring me back into the fold, much as I would have liked to see Oak Hill again."

"And your name?"

Race chuckled. "Another sentimental gesture. Hank asked my mom to name the baby after him—which is pretty nervy if you ask me, since he wasn't even going to marry her. But she *hated* the name Henry. So, instead, I'm Race."

"Did you know he would leave you Oak Hill?"

"No. He never mentioned it. I guess I wasn't entirely surprised. I knew it held unhappy memories for his wife, and his kids probably had no real use for it. I didn't think he'd leave such a valuable piece of property to his wayward bastard son. Still, he was given to sentimental gestures. In fact, you were the only real surprise. Finding myself co-owning the place with a stranger, and a beautiful one at that.''

Vicky felt her cheeks grow red, and she tilted her face forward to hide her blush behind a curtain of damp hair. For the very first time in her life she was finding pleasure in being called beautiful. Perhaps it was the way he said it, as if it were an obvious statement of fact rather than a compliment designed to flatter. The last time he'd said it, it had verged on insult....

"What are you thinking about?" Race asked.

"How confusing people are. Kind, generous, brilliant Hank, always lacking courage, getting a woman he perhaps even loved pregnant all those years ago and never knowing how to set it right. And you, always so sure of yourself, always laughing, starting out life without a father and losing your mother. And Eleanore. I always thought of her as some kind of witch, but she had a burden to bear all those years, too, didn't she?''

They were silent for a while, each absorbed in remembering. Finally Vicky got to her feet and suggested they walk back to get the fan he'd asked to borrow. Race shook off his pensive mood and looked speculatively at her.

"And what about you, Vicky? Where did you come from?''

"Oh, everywhere," she said lightly. "My dad is a naval officer. I was born in Singapore, but we lived all over: Asia, Europe, North Africa, Hawaii, sometimes even the good old U.S.A.''

"Did you like it?''

"No. No, I hated it. All of it." She saw from his face that the deadness in her tone surprised him.

"Brothers and sisters?" he asked.

"No. Just me. My mother couldn't have any more after me; too dangerous for her, the doctor said. A great disappointment to my father, who'd always wanted a long line of sons to carry on the navy tradition. So they named me Victoria, more or less after him, when they realized there would never be a Victor. And watching me grow always depressed him, because he could imagine how tall and strong his sons would have been.''

"Victoria?'' Race repeated softly. "No, it doesn't suit you, does it? Vicky is much better.''

"Ironic, isn't it? We were both named after men we don't love and never see. We don't even use the names they wanted to give us.''

"Was it just because he wanted a son?'' Race asked.

"No. It was everything about me. I just never fit in with the strict disciplines of a military life.''

"I can believe that.'' One side of Race's mouth lifted in a slight smile.

"A lot of military men are perfectly ordinary fathers. Mine just had a lot of hang-ups. He thought affection and emotion were weak. So no one hugged or kissed anyone else without being criticized. I was never allowed to cry or show my fear or be open about my feelings. Everything in our house was run on rigid lines of discipline and efficiency and obedience and proper conduct. He was never intentionally cruel. He just treated me like a sailor. Only I wasn't a sailor; I was a daughter.''

"Where was your mom?''

"Right there. Busy being the woman behind the man, helping his career, being the perfect officer's wife. They made a great team. The only way she ever let him down was by not giving him sons. *I*, on the other hand, have let him down every day since I was born.''

"So how did you become such an animal lover? Was it to get away from them?''

"Partly. And partly because I didn't have many friends as a kid. We moved around so much I never got to know other kids very well. And then, I was a tall, plain, skinny tomboy and shy and gawky, and kids can be very nasty. But everywhere we went there were stray cats and dogs that would be my friends right away and never hurt or reject or turn on me.

"So I got interested in them. When I was eighteen I left my parents' house and went to college to study zoology.

After college I joined the Peace Corps. I wanted to do something useful, and I didn't really have anywhere to go. They sent me to India for two and a half years. When I came back to the States I decided it was time to settle down—for the first time in my life.''

"So what did you do then?"

"There's not a whole lot you can do with just one degree in zoology. I started thinking about going to grad school and getting more specialized, but to be honest I didn't really want to go back to school. I was working on an animal-rescue project when I met Hank. That's when the idea for a kennel was taking shape in my head. I found out about the land and told Hank about my ideas, and he became interested, too. So we became partners. He put up all the money. I put in all the work.... It's the first place I've ever called home.''

She trailed off, surprised at herself. She didn't often talk about her past, and almost never at such length. Race was staring pensively at the ground, but she knew he'd been listening. What was he thinking about? He seemed to be brooding on something extremely unpleasant.

"So Hank kept you a secret all these years?" she murmured.

"More or less. His family knows about me. A few of his friends. My grandfather and local people knew. Obviously Wade knows. As a kid I was so ashamed my father didn't want me, I never told anybody who he was. As an adult, I've always told the essential truth: I haven't got a father. His name's on my birth certificate, though, and a few other documents, but presumably it's such an ordinary name that no one ever guessed. Until now.''

"Until now?"

"Look, Vicky, I've kept quiet, but I never tried to *hide* it. Why should I? It was his mistake. I'm not going to cover it up for him. Already his lawyers and your staff and God knows how many local people know who I am. How long before word spreads?"

"Do you mind?"

"As long as people don't ask insulting questions about my mom, why should I mind? I'm not ashamed of it. It's a bit rough on Eleanore, though."

"What do you mean, rough on Eleanore?" Vicky demanded.

"Well, it's bound to be pretty humiliating for her if her friends start whispering about me and putting two and two together. But then, that's typical of Hank. None of it can hurt him now, so with a magnanimous and generous gesture, he throws the rest of us in at the deep end. You included. For a guy who was brilliant at his career, he sure made a mess of his personal life."

This time it was Vicky's turn to stare at the grass as they walked side by side. What a tangle Hank's past was, still playing itself out in the present. He'd left them all behind to finish the game without him. All except Race's mother.

"She must have been a very brave woman," Vicky said.

"My mom? She was," he answered with a reminiscent smile. "Never bitter, either. She loved Hank, but she knew him for what he was and accepted it. Then she went out and made her own life."

"I thought I knew him for what he was. But I guess I still don't understand people very well."

Race made no answer to that, and they continued along the grassy bank in silence. The soft grass tickled Vicky's bare feet pleasantly. The air was hot; the breeze was scented with wild mint and lilac; the sound of rustling leaves and plants floated on the wind. Eden minus the Serpent, she mused. Or was Race the serpent, moving in smoothly to change her perceptions, to feed her from the tree of knowledge? There was more to it than that, she thought as she studied him from under her lashes. Something about the man himself was fundamentally disturbing, unpredictable and intriguing. He was nothing like his father. And yet that was not entirely true, either, since he possessed all of Hank's charm and winning ways with people.

So was he the serpent in paradise, or were they playing Cain and Abel together? And who was who?

Experiencing a strange prickling sensation Vicky looked down. As if her metaphors had come to life, her feet came to rest on a long, thin, smoothly scaled, warm body. The snake sluggishly raised its head and let its sharp-toothed jaws weave closer to Vicky's bare ankle. Without thinking, she shrieked at the top of her lungs and threw her arms around Race.

"What the—?"

"Snake! Snake! It's a snake!" Vicky gibbered.

"Oh, yes. So it is," he agreed mildly, looking in the direction of her wild gesticulations. Her sudden move had startled the snake into slithering rapidly away before Race could see its menacing pose. "What kind?"

"I don't know! I don't care! I *hate* snakes!" She shuddered violently and clutched Race more tightly. He obligingly put his arms around her and dragged her a few feet away from the spot and into the shade of an old oak tree.

"I find it ironic that you of all people should be afraid of a little thing like that." Race's voice was amused, but his arms held her tightly and the hand that stroked her red curls was gentle and comforting.

Vicky was trembling and panting. Her teeth chattered and horrified little moans escaped her lips as she buried her face against Race's shoulder.

"Hey, you really are spooked, aren't you?" He sounded concerned.

"Oh, they're horrible creatures, horrible! I was bitten by one in India—"

"Poisonous?"

"Yes. And it hurt so much! I was delirious for days...." She shuddered again. "But I've always hated them, always. Even before that, when I was working at the Children's Zoo, I could never *touch* the boa constrictor. There's something so horrible about the way they look and feel, the way they twist and wriggle and glide around without any legs, the way they swallow living things whole. Do you know they have no eyelids, and they can't ever close their eyes? There's something about them that's just so insidious, so— so *evil*!" she finished, knowing she sounded hysterical.

"You shall bruise his head and he shall bruise your heel— or words to that effect?" Race said dryly. Vicky shivered. His arms tightened around her. "Easy, easy. He's gone now," he assured her.

He held her against his chest and touched her hair with a tender, rhythmic stroke as if she were a frightened animal, murmuring soothing words to her all the while.

Vicky calmed down after a bit. She sighed and nestled contentedly in his arms, enjoying the brief respite of being protected by a body even stronger and taller than her own; it was a strange sensation and not at all an unpleasant one. She rubbed her face against the soft khaki of his shirt. His golden skin smelled so good; a warm, earthy, male smell. She slightly loosened her frantic, panic-stricken grip around his neck; he hadn't complained, but she must have very nearly strangled him. Her hand brushed his wavy hair, and now she deliberately twined her fingers in it, enjoying its thick, coarse texture. The scent and feel of him, his warmth surrounding her, the steady beat of his heart against her chest, all created a hypnotic effect that lulled her into a limp, drowsy state of mind.

His hand ceased stroking her hair to smooth down her back. He kissed her temple, and both his hands moved slowly, exploring her body, the shape of her hips, the smoothness of the arms that held him, the strong muscles of her back. Her T-shirt provided very little obstruction, and she could feel the warmth and strength of those gentle hands. She sighed deeply.

Something in Race seemed to break free at the sound of that voluptuous sigh. He tightened his arms convulsively around her and buried his face in her thick red hair to plant hot kisses on her neck. Vicky tensed for a moment in surprise and confusion, and then something awoke in her as well, a fire she didn't recognize and couldn't control. Her head tilted sideways of its own volition and her mouth sought the tender place just below his ear, which tasted warm and salty. Race shuddered violently, and his kisses and caresses became more feverish.

"You've been driving me crazy. Do you know that?" he muttered in a burning, unsteady voice.

"I—I have?" Her own voice was weak and breathless.

His hands were everywhere, sliding through her hair, roughly stroking her cheek, massaging her back, smoothing over her round bottom to press her hips closer to his. She rubbed her face against his neck, moving her head to one side to give his hot, firm lips access to her shoulder. He roughly pulled at her neckline and kissed her pale flesh with intense concentration, his warm mouth tasting, his tongue lightly teasing. Vicky's breath came out in a rush and she squeezed her eyes shut.

"Yes, you have," he growled against her ear before nipping it teasingly. "Swimming naked right outside my window every morning, sunning yourself on the grass like Neptune's daughter, walking around every day in those short shorts and skimpy T-shirts, sweating till you shine like your body was oiled. Smiling at every customer, hugging every stray cat and dog—and refusing to even speak to me!"

He sounded so irritated with her, Vicky had to laugh. He gripped her shoulders and roughly shoved her away a bit to scowl into her face. But as he looked into her laughing eyes he was forced to grin reluctantly.

"And I thought you were hard at work all this time," she teased him.

"I have been. It's the only way I could keep my mind off of ravishing you," Race admitted.

She reached up to touch his smooth, strong jaw. Here, in the shade, the sun couldn't find him to play with the gold in his hair and he looked dark, dark and sensual, a warm stranger come to pull her into secret shadows.

"You've lost your halo," she murmured.

"No, but I'm about to," he said softly. He slid his fingers into her hair to pull her head back gently. He lowered his face to hers, his eyes taking in every detail of her passionate expression.

He brushed his mouth across hers teasingly again and again, his touch feather light, his eyes half-closed and heavy lidded with passion. Vicky pulled against the restraining pressure of the hand wrapped in her long hair to brush her open mouth against his cheek and taste his warm skin with her tongue. They teased each other endlessly in the hot shadows, as if they were engaged in a contest to see who could torment the other most with half caresses and butterfly kisses.

Race won, and Vicky yanked away from his restraining hand as she wrapped her arms around his neck and pressed her open mouth firmly against his. He seemed happy to cooperate, however, and wrapped her in a tight embrace as he hungrily returned her fierce kisses, barely pausing to snatch breath between each one.

One strong brown hand stroked her ribs then moved around to firmly cup a full, heavy breast. With his thumb he stroked and teased the taut peak till it ached. Vicky moaned and pressed herself wildly into his hand. She stroked his hair, his face, his neck, his broad shoulders, transported beyond the awareness of anything except his touch and the need to touch him.

Their lips met again and their tongues moved along each other exploringly, languidly, tasting the mystery of a new lover. Vicky's knees gave way, and it was only the strength of Race's arms that kept her standing.

He looked down into her face, his eyes smoky with sensuality and desire. He moved his hand from her breast to stroke her firm thighs where her long shirt had hiked up.

"I want you," he whispered. His expression sought an answer to the unasked question.

Vicky was a creature of impulse, and there was no question in her mind as to what she wanted at this moment. She opened her mouth to tell him—

"Vicky!" It was Ginny's voice shouting down the path from the cottage. "Vicky! Vicky!" Louder now, already twenty feet nearer.

Vicky came to her senses in a rush and yanked herself out of Race's arms as if he'd slapped her. She leaned against the tree trunk for support, since her legs were still wobbly, and stared at Race as if he were the devil himself.

Ginny's voice was only a few yards away now.

"Over here, Ginny," Vicky called weakly.

Ginny slipped through the leafy veil of a low-hanging branch. She took in Vicky's flushed face and glittering eyes as she leaned weakly against the tree trunk and Race's closed, dark expression. "What the heck is going on here?"

"She thought she saw a snake," Race answered smoothly. "I was just showing her there's nothing to be afraid of."

Vicky shot him a fierce glare, which he returned with a brooding, speculative look.

"Oh, Vicky, honey," Ginny said, giving her a maternal hug. "Poor kid. It's the one thing she can't handle. You know, she nearly died of a snakebite once," Ginny told Race.

"Why did you come looking for me, Ginny?" Vicky asked tiredly.

"There's big trouble at the kennel. You'd better get changed and come right away. You, too, Race—we may need all the help we can get."

"I'll be right there," said Vicky, trying to pull her confused senses together.

The three of them stepped out into the hot sunlight and started up the path away from the river, Ginny in the lead.

"Your guardian angel coming to the rescue, Vicky?" Race asked softly.

The sun was glinting down on his dark head, highlighting the gold and giving him back his halo.

"Funny that you of all people should say that," Vicky retorted, and turned to hurry up the path after Ginny.

Four

Vicky arrived at the kennel less than ten minutes later, suitably attired for work: blue jeans, sneakers, a T-shirt and a ponytail. Race tagged along at her heels, quiet and pensive. Ginny had left her alone with him at the cottage and gone back to the kennel, so Vicky still didn't know the nature of the problem.

The parking area was full of cars, and about a dozen customers, some with pets and some without, were standing around on the front lawn. Quite a few of Vicky's staff were standing outside as well, including Ginny; her son, Brian; Nadine and Rebecca, one of the college kids Vicky had hired.

"What's going on?" Vicky asked Ginny.

"Am I glad to see you!" said Rebecca. She was bleeding profusely while Brian inexpertly bandaged her hand.

"What happened to you? Why's everybody standing out here?"

"There's a crazy dog loose somewhere in the kennel," answered Ginny.

"What?"

"About twenty minutes ago this guy—" Ginny gestured to a nervous, well-dressed man about Race's age "—brought in a German shepherd without a leash."

"Did you put a leash on it?" Everyone at Oak Hill carried sturdy slip ropes to use as leashes; Vicky had always stressed that every dog had to have a leash, even if it was only going from one room to the next.

"I tried to put a leash on him," said Rebecca, grimly indicating her bloody hand. "He didn't like the idea."

Ginny continued the explanation. "So I asked this man if he would take the dog back to his run himself, to avoid someone else getting nailed. And in the back hall the dog freaked out and went for me. Luckily he just nicked me." She showed Vicky some angry scratches on her leg. "But then this guy—" Ginny glared fiercely at the nervous man "—let him go and he ran off."

"Oh, no," Vicky said. It was the heat of the day, and every door in the back hall and the four kennel wings was left open in the hope of catching every possible breeze.

Every run was private, so the German shepherd couldn't come in contact with another dog. The whole complex was surrounded by a very high chain-link fence, so he couldn't possibly run away. But he was back there somewhere in several thousand square yards of space full of blind corners, sharp curves, dead ends and a maze of aisles and hallways.

She raised her head and met Race's eyes. He still had a limited knowledge of the kennel, but she knew he was familiar enough with its area and their working procedures to follow her thoughts.

"Oh, no," he agreed grimly.

Vicky turned to the nervous customer. "The best thing, sir, would be for you to go inside with me and try to calm down your dog—"

"He's not my dog," said the man apologetically.

"Well, where's his owner?" she demanded.

"At this moment? Somewhere over the Atlantic Ocean, I'm afraid—on his way to Europe. I'm his personal assistant. He left rather suddenly on an emergency trip and asked me to bring his dog here for him right away."

"Who are we talking about?"

The man named an important State Department official, a friend of Hank's. Vicky closed her eyes and let out a string of invective remarkable for its originality and vigor. Even Race looked surprised.

She vividly remembered the dog in question. Its neurotic, hysterically vicious temperament was encouraged by its owner, who mistakenly perceived it as a sign of loyalty rather than as a behavior disorder. Even the man's family couldn't go near the dog on most occasions. Vicky had agreed to board it whenever he went out of the country, provided—and she had emphasized this—that he always brought the dog in himself. Brian had once gone in the yellow pick-up-and-delivery-service van to get the dog, and the animal had tried to remove one of his arms.

Vicky had all the facilities to care for a vicious dog—provided it didn't run away from its owner before it even reached its dog run! The setup at Oak Hill made it possible for the staff to feed, clean and look after a dog without ever coming into physical contact with him if he seemed likely to attack.

Even this supposedly foolproof system could occasionally be hazardous, as the scars on Vicky's arms and legs testified. Working with live animals, one could always count on the unexpected to happen. No system could be perfect, she thought grimly, as she looked at the abandoned kennel.

The qualities that had made Hank believe in her enough to sink a small fortune into her project came to the fore now. She gently took Rebecca's mangled hand from Brian and, with skillful hands, stopped the bleeding, disinfected the wound and bandaged the bite while her mind worked furiously and she snapped out orders to her staff.

"Ginny, go to the garage and get as many folding chairs as you can find; set them up in the shade for the customers.

Rebecca, go to my house. There's a pitcher of orange juice and some lemonade. Bring them both here and offer everyone a cold drink. Brian, I want you to find me that iron leash—you know the one I mean?''

"Yeah. Do you want the gloves, too?'' They sometimes used heavy welders' gloves to protect their hands from being bitten or scratched. Vicky also used them to clean Mrs. Periwinkle's cage.

"No, I'm too clumsy in those things.''

Brian, Ginny and Rebecca dashed off to their appointed tasks.

"Nadine,'' Vicky said, "make sure all the water pressure's on high, in case he corners me.'' Her efficient staff was soon doing its best to make the customers comfortable in the shade, and all were surprisingly pleasant and understanding as Vicky apologized for the inconvenience. Race lounged casually against a tree trunk, but Vicky wasn't fooled; there was an animal alertness in every line of his long body, and his gaze was fixed on her.

Brian brought her the iron leash and she tested it quickly. "Give me your slip rope in case I drop mine.''

"Do you want me to help you?''

"No, thanks, Brian. You know the rules; I don't pay you enough to get bitten.''

In fact, every one of her staff wanted to help her, but she was adamant in her refusal.

"You all know damned well that the more of us there are, the more frightened he'll be. Just keep an eye on the outside wings and give a shout if you see him.''

"You'll catch him easier with at least one person helping you, Vicky,'' Ginny insisted.

"If it looks certain I can't catch him alone, I'll let one of you come back there,'' Vicky conceded, "but I'd rather try it alone first.'' She grinned. "But who knows? A few scars might give your son some character, Ginny. And some women find scars sexy.'' Brian scowled at her.

Race followed Vicky around to the side door and grabbed her arm as she tried to go inside.

"That looks like a weapon," he said, indicating the iron leash.

"It's not. I don't use weapons on animals." She was insulted. She showed him how it worked. A thick, flexible cord ran through a long metal tube, forming a handle at one end and a noose at the other. The idea was to slip the noose over the dog's head and pull on the handle to tighten it like a leash. The iron bar served to ensure that once the dog was on the leash, he couldn't get any closer to Vicky. It effectively gave her control of a vicious dog without hurting him in any way. Of course, one had to be very strong to use it.

"Very clever," said Race. "But if you miss your aim?"

"Let's hope I don't." She tried to open the door to go inside. Her way was suddenly blocked by an arm that seemed to be made of steel and whipcord.

"I'm not letting you go in there alone, Vicky," he said firmly.

"I can't let any of the others come with me. I really *don't* pay them enough to get hurt. Hank and I agreed that if anything like this happened—"

"Then damn Hank for letting you do things like this!"

"It's my job, Race. It goes with the territory. It's part of being the boss. And while I'm scared witless and would much rather let someone else do this, I don't have any choice," she said steadily.

"Then I'm coming with you."

"You can't. You don't know the layout of the kennel well enough to help me, and you don't know how to behave around a hysterical dog," she protested as he took Brian's slip rope from her back pocket. "You'll just wind up getting yourself bitten."

"Maybe," he agreed grimly. "But since I'm your partner now, it would seem to be my job, too, wouldn't it?"

"Race—"

"You'd better just explain what you want me to do."

She looked into those gray eyes, which were hard and steely now, and realized she had finally come up against a will as strong as her own. She could see nothing would change his mind, so she acquiesced. Instead of feeling annoyed at his interference, she was strangely grateful for his concern and his help. He was confident and competent, and her task would indeed be easier with two people.

"Okay." She swiftly explained everything to him as best she could. They cautiously entered the back hallway together and quickly searched it. There was no sign of the dog.

"He must be somewhere in the wings. Just remember that at this point he's confused and scared, and that makes him very dangerous and unpredictable," she warned.

They separated and began patrolling the kennel wings, indoors and outdoors. The object was to encourage the dog—Captain—to go into an empty run. Once he was in a run with the door shut behind him, they could give him food and water, arrange his indoor run comfortably and sort out the paperwork. Then everything could return to normal. With this end in mind, Race and Vicky opened the door of every empty run they passed to give Captain plenty of opportunities to enter one.

Vicky could hear the dogs barking frantically in the next wing over, which meant something exciting was happening. She turned the corner and saw Captain trotting up and down. As soon as he saw her he raced straight for her, teeth bared, snarling viciously. Somewhere behind her, outside the compound, Brian shouted, "Vicky!"

Caught by surprise and facing a 150-pound dog rushing at her with its teeth bared, Vicky let her instincts for self-preservation take over. She dropped the iron leash, grabbed the chain-link fence and climbed to the roof with a speed and strength she doubted she could ever match again. She jerked her foot up just before a dozen shiny, sharp teeth could sink into it. She sat looking down at the leaping, snarling dog, nervously wondering just how high he could jump with his adrenaline pumping so furiously.

Race came tearing around the far corner, alerted by the shouts of her staff outside the fence and the frantic barking of the dogs within.

"Vicky!" he shouted.

Race ran toward them, his face an expression of mingled fury and alarm.

"Stay back!" Vicky shouted.

But something in Race's expression must have frightened even the dog who abandoned his captive audience and ran off.

"Are you all right?" Race asked, helping Vicky climb down from the roof.

"Yes, yes, I'm fine. But he's scared witless, poor guy."

"You're crazy. You know that?" asked Race in exasperation.

"So are you, running straight into his jaws like that."

"I guess I lost my head when I saw him going for you," Race admitted.

"Look, you go that way and I'll go this way. We've got him narrowed down to two wings now."

They separated and continued the search. Vicky slipped cautiously through an indoor wing, opening doors to empty runs as she went and reaching through the chain-link fence to reassuringly pet the boarders. They were very excited by the whole adventure and seemed to be having a great time, she thought wryly.

Overhead on the speakers a popular rock singer was singing a song that was one of her favorites, but today it hit too close to home:

You've been bitten once before,
You're still feelin' pretty sore,
You'll forget him wait and see,
'Cause I'm gonna make you think about me!
I know that once bit is twice shy. . . .

"Yes, indeed," muttered Vicky, fingering an old scar on her arm. She heard a ferocious bark outside and a shout followed by some vigorous cursing. She ran outside and rounded the corner, and her heart nearly stopped at what she saw.

Race was standing against the dead end of the farthest right-hand aisle. His left arm was bleeding profusely. The German shepherd stood about ten feet in front of him, effectively blocking his escape. Its whole body vibrated with angry growling.

Race stood stock-still, a dynamic tension gripping his whole body. He spoke calmly to the dog in a low, soothing voice. When he saw her he gave her a quick, reassuring grin and said hopefully, "Barking dogs never bite?"

"Race!" Vicky croaked. "How did—"

"Ironically enough, he was sniffing around in an empty run. I didn't see him till I tripped over him." The runs had solid steel sides from the ground to waist level, effectively blocking one's view.

Captain looked from Race to Vicky with a trapped, panic-stricken expression.

"Don't try to touch him," she warned.

"I hadn't planned on it," was the dry response.

"Don't look directly into his eyes; it's taken as a challenge. Don't make any sudden moves. Don't show any fear." She tried to dredge up any knowledge that could help him.

"Do you have any suggestions about what I *should* do?" he asked reasonably.

She thought frantically. "Yes, yes. There's a faucet overhead, about three feet in front of you. If you turn it on, water will start gushing out and he won't cross through that. Move very slowly."

Moving with a slow, stealthy animal grace, Race took two steps forward. As he reached up to turn on the faucet, there was a terrible moment when Vicky was sure Captain was going to leap for him. Then Race's hand moved and suddenly water was gushing out of the pipes and into the aisle, splashing over Race and hitting Captain in the face. Startled into action, the dog spun around and, sliding across the wet pavement, headed straight for Vicky.

Race shouted her name and went running after him. His foot slipped on the smooth, wet surface, and he flew up in the air and landed in a sprawling heap—which, inappropriately, struck Vicky as hysterically funny.

She stood her ground, hoping she'd slip the iron leash over Captain's head on the first try, since it didn't look as though she'd get a second chance. She missed. Her heart leaped as Captain barreled into her and knocked her onto her back. He didn't even pause, but sped over her prostrate body and into an empty run directly behind her. She rolled over immediately and slammed the door behind him. Then she collapsed facedown onto the ground, sweating and trembling, trying to catch her breath—for he had stepped on her stomach.

A moment later Race hauled her fiercely to her feet and wrapped her in a fierce embrace. His mouth moved over her face and hair in rough, punishing kisses.

"I'll kill you if you ever do anything like this again," he said harshly.

Vicky leaned against him weakly. Suddenly, inexplicably, she started to laugh. Race released his viselike grip to pull back and look into her face in astonishment. His bemused expression only fed the fire, and tears rolled down her cheeks as she laughed even harder.

"If you could only have seen yourself," she gasped, "fly up in the air and then go *splat*! I'm sorry, Race. I shouldn't laugh." And she laughed some more.

She didn't know whether it was his sense of humor that took hold or the release of tension, but suddenly Race, too, was laughing.

The staff found them a few moments later, covered with sweat, blood and water, guffawing like a couple of lunatics and holding each other up.

"I'm glad you think it's so funny," snapped Ginny in disgust. "I thought you were both dog food there for a minute."

"It's Vicky; she's hysterical," explained Race seriously, and burst out laughing again.

They calmed down after a few minutes and went into the lounge, where Vicky treated Race's arm after giving orders that Captain should get special care that day in view of his harrowing experience.

"You're crazy," Race murmured. "He could have killed you out there, and now you want to throw something extra into his food bowl?"

"I may not like him personally," Vicky said as she cleaned and disinfected the nasty bite on Race's arm, "but he isn't responsible. Anyone that vicious was obviously born pretty mixed up, but his owner is the real culprit. He has encouraged and exacerbated this neurotic behavior. German shepherds are strong willed. If they're not raised properly, they can turn out to be vicious, or friendly but so rambunctious that no normal household can put up with them."

"All right. Point taken." Race sighed in resignation.

"People, on the other hand, are entirely different," Vicky continued.

"Oh?"

"Yes. Obviously everyone's influenced to some extent by their environment, but in the end a person is entirely responsible for his own behavior. I am convinced that you, for instance—" She jerked her head away as he stroked her hair.

"Yes?"

"Would have been wicked and impertinent no matter who raised you." She removed his hand from her thigh.

"I see." He traced the fine bones of her hand.

"Are you listening to me?"

"More or less." His hand came up to her chin, to tilt it up for his kiss.

"Race!" She grabbed both his hands and pushed them firmly away from her. He winced slightly, since her grip on his injured arm was very rough.

"Sorry," she mumbled.

"That's okay. I'm getting rather used to your impulsive ways. What is it you want to say?"

His eyes were clear and candid as she watched her. Getting lost in their depths, she nearly forgot what she wanted to say. "I'm very grateful to you for helping me today," she began, proud of having regained her composure, "especially since you didn't have to and I would have had a very rough time if you hadn't been there. I'm sorry you got hurt in the process."

"But?" he probed.

"But what...happened this morning by the river was a mistake, and we shouldn't...let it happen again. Surely you must see that under the circumstances, any kind of... entanglement between us isn't a good idea."

"I've never heard you use so many euphemisms in one breath," he said mockingly. "Losing your nerve? What is it you really want to say, Vicky?"

"I want you to keep your hands off me!" she snapped, stung into a sharp reply.

"Do you really?"

"Yes!" She was irritated that he'd once again made her lose her temper. She tried to speak more calmly. "Yes, I do. And, of course, I'll stop swimming in the nude if you find it so...distracting."

Race's face didn't change, but his eyes grew hard and speculative. Vicky lowered her gaze. She knew she was hotheaded, emotional and impulsive by nature, and she was learning that Race was very clever and adaptable. And for that reason she was absolutely not going to let him get into a position where he might be able to influence her decisions. Not under the circumstances. Down by the riverside she had discovered something dangerous: the first man in her life who was excited by her strength instead of intimidated by it, who encouraged her wildness to catch fire instead of dousing it, who fed her passions with his own. That the man who held that enthralling, tantalizing weapon in his power should be Race, of all people, alarmed Vicky no end. Better to keep her distance. Better for Oak Hill and her future.

"What are you thinking now, I wonder," Race said pensively.

"I'm trying to decide how much dog food to order for next month," she lied.

Race laughed. "You're very hard on a man's ego, Vicky. But luckily mine is pretty unbruisable," he confided.

"I can believe that," she answered churlishly.

"Vicky? Here you are! The girls have just told me what happened! Are you all right?"

Race watched as a good-looking man in his early thirties came into the room. As Vicky stood up to greet him, he took both her hands in his and studied her face with gentle concern.

"I'm fine," Vicky assured him. "Race, this is Dean Alexander. He's a local vet. Dean, Race is sort of my new partner." The two men shook hands, but Race gave no greeting.

"Yes. I've heard of you, of course, Race," said Dean. If he noticed Race's stiff attitude he gave no sign of it; his manner was warm and welcoming. "Can't keep something like that quiet around here. A lot of the older residents around here remember your family and say they were fine people. It's good to see you back here. I'm glad Hank left Oak Hill to the two people who would cherish it most."

Even in his stubborn mood, Race couldn't ignore the sincere friendliness of the other man's welcome. He thanked him politely.

"What brings you out this way, Dean?" asked Vicky.

"Two things. I wanted to talk to you about parvo virus before you get swamped with customers this summer and to tell Nadine about some new flea-and-tick dip."

"Good. I'd like my whole staff to hear what you have to say, actually."

"Right. And the other matter is purely personal. Would you like to go out for dinner Thursday?"

"Thursday? Yes, I'm sure Thursday's fine. Why don't you go join Ginny in the office and I'll tell Nadine you're here."

"Okay," Dean agreed, and left the room.

Race grabbed Vicky's arm as she tried to follow.

"Are you really going to go out with that guy?" he asked in a low voice.

"Of course I am. You just heard me say so, didn't you? Why shouldn't I go out with him? He's nice; he's fun; he's attractive; he's interesting—"

"Sure, if you want to talk about fleas and viruses."

"Those happen to be things that concern me," she said angrily. "And if you find them that dull, why don't you go and find someone you can discuss nails and hammers and planking with?" She yanked her arm away from him.

"I think I'll go do just that." He stalked out of the room.

Vicky's gaze followed after him, her emotions churning and tumbling inside her, contradictory and chaotic.

The weather kept heating up in the following weeks. Mist collected on the windows of Vicky's air-conditioned cottage and on the windows of the air-conditioned portions of the kennel. In the wings, the fans and air coolers worked round the clock to maintain a comfortable atmosphere. Sometimes at night steam rose from the damp Virginia soil, giving the land an eerie, unreal look.

Brian was in love. The girl's name was, appropriately enough, Désirée. She was one of the girls Vicky had hired for summer. Désirée was young, ripe, brunette, tanned and beautiful in every respect. What perhaps made her especially attractive was her wardrobe or, rather, lack of one. She worked every day in tight, skimpy hot pants, a bikini top and nothing else. Vicky didn't care what Désirée wore, as long as she did her work. And it was hot, doing hard work outside all day. Men could take their shirts off, and Vicky didn't blame her for emulating this custom as closely as was socially acceptable. Brian was clearly all in favor of the idea. Vicky was amused to note that since Désirée's arrival on the scene, she was getting double her money's worth out of Brian, since, in addition to doing all his own chores, he made a point of finding extra jobs that needed doing wherever Désirée happened to be working.

But although Brian's heart clearly belonged to Désirée, his eyes were enjoying a summer feast, since all the woman at Oak Hill had adapted their attire to suit the sultry days, though perhaps not as severely as Désirée had.

Vicky was standing out in the hot sun with Brian, looking over the tractor. She wore only old sandals, short cutoffs and a T-shirt she had altered to leave her arms, neck and stomach bare. Her red mane was piled carelessly on top of her head. She was frowning at the moment.

"Would you please look at my face and try to concentrate on the conversation, Brian?"

His eyes lifted quickly to her face. "Sorry, Vic, I just...um..."

"This tractor is brand-new. Are you trying to tell me something's wrong with it already?" she asked impatiently.

"Nothing serious. But sometimes, in third gear, the stick shift gets stuck and it takes a while to get her to stop."

"But you always do get it to stop."

"Sure."

"Okay. I should have some more cash on Monday. You can get it sorted out then. Ask...ask Race to help you."

"Help him what?" Race said behind her.

Vicky whirled to face him. Their relationship for the past two weeks had been strained and uneasy, and she had taken care not to speak to him if she could avoid it. All things considered, she didn't like asking him for help. On the other hand, she couldn't afford to waste more money.

She asked him to look at the tractor. He figured out the problem pretty quickly and told Brian exactly what was needed.

"Well, at least she doesn't steer wild like the old one, hey, Vicky?" Brian said cheerfully.

"No," Vicky agreed. She explained to Race, "Brian broke his arm on the old one last year."

"Yeah. I turned left, it swung wild, and I fell on my head. Vicky here claims that's when I first started showing signs of lunacy."

"Or merely adolescence..." added Vicky.

A big rented trailer-truck pulled into the drive and started maneuvering to back up to the side entrance of the kennel.

"That'll be Ginny with the dog food," Vicky said.

"Dog food?" echoed Race.

"Mm-hmm. Five thousand pounds of dry meal packed in fifty-pound bags."

Ginny finished parking, opened the back doors, pulled out the ramp and went inside the kennel to roust everyone out.

"Get along, Brian. I've got work to do," Vicky said.

"I'm mowing down at the river stretch if you need me," he replied, and drove off in the tractor.

"Want help?" Race asked Vicky.

"Sure. If you don't mind," she said noncommittally.

As Rebecca, Désirée and Nadine piled out the door and headed for the truck, a regular customer stopped Vicky in the driveway. "Vicky, surely you're not gonna let these little girls unload that big truck by themselves? Haven't you got a few strong fellows to do it? Here, let me give you a hand."

Vicky looked at the little man's potbelly, swayback and red face. It was only with great difficulty that she kept herself from remarking that the last thing she needed was for a man to throw out his bad back or have a heart attack when she had so much work to do. Instead, she lectured him on one of her favorite topics while Race watched in amused silence.

"I would first like to point out, Mr. Lyons, that women are physically better designed than men for carrying heavy weights, particularly over a long distance or long period of time. The heaviest part of a woman's body is her hips, which provides for a more even weight distribution when she carries something on her shoulders."

"But—" Mr. Lyons tried to interrupt.

"In fact, in most undeveloped societies today, it is still the woman who bears heavy weights."

"But—"

"And since it is a medical fact that labor and childbirth are the hardest physical work any human body ever does, unloading five thousand pounds of dog food should seem relatively mild in comparison."

"Yes, of course, Vicky," said Mr. Lyons resignedly.

Taking a leaf from Race's book, Vicky gave the little man her most winning smile and said, "But I appreciate the offer, sir."

Mr. Lyons nodded and smiled back, looking rather pleased.

As Vicky stalked away gracefully she heard Race say behind her, "I'd take her word for it, sir. She's carrying all fifty acres of Oak Hill on those soft shoulders, and she looks pretty healthy to me." He gave the man a friendly clap on the back and followed Vicky.

Unloading the food truck was a familiar job at Oak Hill, so they all worked quickly and efficiently, chatting and laughing as they did so. Race worked in the truck, passing bags of dry meal down to Vicky, Nadine, Rebecca and Désirée, who carried them into the feed room and put them where Ginny directed.

As the strongest, Vicky took two bags at a time, one hoisted on a shoulder and the other carried under her arm. Race, who had even held that tall body and felt its strength, commented on her stamina.

"I'm used to it," she said simply as they walked back into the kennel with the final load on their shoulders. Désirée was left sweeping out the back of the truck.

Race put down his load in the feed room and moved to take Vicky's. She maintained the one on her shoulder, explaining she would take it into the kitchen for that day's feedings. She realized he wasn't listening. His expression had changed. His eyes had grown smoky, and she knew he was taking in her flushed face, the rise and fall of her breasts under the thin cotton of her T-shirt, her stomach glistening with sweat and the long length of her bare legs. His eyes met hers, and she turned away as if he'd burned her. She wrestled with her own unruly thoughts, for he had taken off his shirt during the unloading; his muscular bronze chest and shoulders gleamed in the sunlight, and when she stood close to him she caught his pleasant, musky scent.

They washed up and enjoyed a pitcher of iced tea with the rest of the staff. The usual laughter and jokes prevailed, even in Brian's absence. Race was fully clothed again, and both he and Vicky were calmer when he asked to speak to her privately.

"I have to go home to get some paperwork. You can talk to me on the way," she said.

"It's about the lawyer," Race said as they walked along the familiar path to her cottage. "I explained the situation to him and got the usual responses: it's highly irregular and so forth. He wants to know if we want a formal agreement in writing."

Vicky stopped abruptly. "I have no reason to want one. But you do."

His candid gray eyes met hers seriously. "We've got a handshake agreement. That's good enough for me," he said evenly.

"Thank you." She was glad that despite the tension between them he respected her integrity. Perhaps too much, since she still wasn't above trying to find ways to hang on to the kennel if things didn't work out....

She lowered her eyes and shifted uncomfortably. She could hear the steady hum of the tractor in the distance.

"Should I trust you?" Race murmured almost to himself. "Look at me, Vicky." She did. "You don't know, either, do you?"

She shifted again, fidgeting. His hand forced her chin up so their eyes met again. There was something else in his look now, something she didn't understand.

"Maybe it's none of my business, but I can't help asking," he said grimly. "What exactly was there between you and—"

Suddenly there was a shout, then a crash and a splash, then a few more shouts. Then Rebel was barking and ducks were quacking and birds were screeching. Race cursed and ran down the path at top speed, heading toward the river with Vicky at his heels.

Brian was treading water and looking in dismay at the tractor, which stood nose down in the river, three-quarters of it submerged in the lapping green water.

"Brian! What happened?" Vicky cried, gaping at him.

"I told you, man. Sometimes it just won't come out of third gear—in time."

Five

Luckily the damage to the tractor was relatively minor, and it would only have to spend a few days in the repair shop. Vicky's warranty didn't cover the cost of towing the tractor out of rivers in case of malfunction, but Race had proved enormously helpful in saving her meager budget; he had pulled the machine out of the river by harnessing it up to the old tractor, with Brian's help, and hauling it out to the cheers of her staff, who by now regarded him as something of a hero. Rebecca even liked to compare her scar with his, since they had both been ''blooded'' on the same day.

Brian shamefacedly offered to give up tractor privileges for the rest of the summer and just work in the kennel, but since Vicky was the one who had let him ride off on a malfunctioning machine, she couldn't allow that. Besides, she saw the way his eyes followed Désirée when he made his humble offer and guessed that he wasn't being entirely noble—or truthful. She wondered if trouble was brewing there.

During the days that followed, Vicky and Race enjoyed an uneasy truce. They no longer deliberately avoided each other, but they also couldn't ignore the tension, both professional and sexual, that seemed to exist constantly between them. And struggling with her feelings for one man made Vicky loath to spend an evening in another man's company. The morning that Race drove off to the airport to pick up his visiting stepfather, Vicky called the local veterinarian and postponed their date for the third time. As she had feared, Dean expressed disappointment but immediately and eagerly suggested another night for their date. Vicky agreed weakly, then spent the rest of the morning working in the office while she wondered how she could get out of this date without offending the friendly and competent veterinarian—and wondering *why* she wanted so desperately to get out of a date with such a man.

"Well, I'll be a son of a gun! Is that thing a dog?"

Vicky turned to see a rugged-looking man in his sixties enter the office with Race. He was staring in fascination at the small ball of animated fur on Vicky's desk. She laughed at his expression.

"Yes. That's Buffy. She's a long-haired Chihuahua."

"Will she get any bigger—or, rather, less small?" the man asked.

"Yes. She's only four months old; she'll probably double in size."

"That still won't be much."

"No," Vicky agreed. "She looked so lost rattling around in that big dog run, I thought I'd bring her out here and spoil her a little. She's so small that just running from one side of the desk to the other exhausts her." Buffy attacked a pencil with enthusiasm.

"She's a cute little thing."

"And she's very well behaved." Buffy made a puddle. "Usually," Vicky added wryly.

"Vicky, this is my partner, Wade Johnson," said Race.

"You'll excuse me if I don't shake your hand at the moment." She and Race smiled at each other, remembering their first meeting.

"No. I see your point," Wade said, chuckling.

Vicky went to wash up and then came back with glasses of iced tea for all three of them. They chatted easily in the air-conditioned office while Wade played with Buffy.

Watching Race from under her lashes, Vicky noticed the obvious respect and affection between him and his stepfather and felt glad for it. She had found a second father in Hank, and it seemed only fair that his real son had also found a father figure in someone.

She glanced out the window as they talked, then said, "Uh-oh, here they come."

"They who?" asked Wade.

"Customers," she answered. "Ginny has a theory that they all wait at the head of the driveway until they've grown into a small herd, then descend on us at once."

Sure enough, five cars came down the drive one after another. As Vicky dealt with them, three more cars arrived and the phone started ringing off the hook.

Race and Wade watched in amusement as Vicky dealt with them all quickly, thoroughly and politely. She checked dogs in, checked dogs out, took reservations, took in grooming customers, gave instructions over the intercom and never once grew flustered or made a mistake.

Finally after a solid twenty-minute rush, the last customer was leaving.

"Thanks, Vicky. I know you'll take good care of him while I'm away."

"Sure will, Mrs. Brown. Have a good trip. See you in two weeks."

With the lobby empty, Vicky sat down at her desk and started entering and deleting information in the computer, scratching instructions on the diet charts and making notes in the reservation book.

"I'm impressed," said Wade.

"No need to be. I created the system. It would be a crying shame if I couldn't operate it efficiently," Vicky replied.

Rebecca entered the room to check one of the lists, then left again without comment. She was soaking from head to foot.

"What on earth happened to that girl?" asked Wade.

"Water fights," Race supplied with a grin.

"Water fights?"

"Sure," Vicky said. "Helps them stay cool, and as long as they get all the hosing done out back, I don't mind."

"Don't mind?" Race teased her. "From what I hear, you're more vicious with a hose than any of them."

"Well...it's fun," she admitted with a grin. "And now that it's so hot, we spend practically all day out there hosing everything down to keep it cool and clean. It can get kind of monotonous."

Race insisted she join him and Wade for lunch at the big house when Ginny came to relieve her. Although the kitchen and bathrooms were still fairly primitive, Vicky had to admit he had been working wonders with the rest of the house. Its true beauty had started to show through as Race cleaned off years' worth of dirt and dust and careless decorating. The living room, where they ate, had been his primary target. Vicky scarcely recognized it. Polished oak floors gleamed beneath the high ceilings. Rotting wood and crumbling plaster had been skillfully repaired or replaced. The drab threadbare curtains had been exchanged for cedar shutters. The walls were painted a fresh, creamy color. The old, musty odors were gone, and the room was cheerful, fresh and bright. He'd gotten rid of the few pieces of shabby furniture that had been in there and was slowly refurnishing it with antiques he'd found locally.

"Where'd you learn to do stuff like this?" Vicky asked Race as she examined a cabinet he was in the process of restoring.

"I had all kinds of jobs during high school and college. I worked for an antique dealer, for a renovator, for a decorator, for a construction company. I picked up a lot of useful things along the way. And a lot of it is just part of my job."

She sat down cross-legged on a beautiful, thick Persian rug that covered most of the floor. "This is great," she said, stroking it.

"Believe it or not, that came out of the attic. It took me days in the hot sun to beat the dust out of it," he said in a blatant bid for sympathy.

"I guess you really have been working hard after all. I never suspected," said Vicky mildly.

"Ah, but all work and no play makes Race a surly fellow," Wade said with a chuckle.

"I play. Don't worry," Race assured him.

"Who with?" Wade asked. Vicky was curious, too. She knew Race sometimes went out in the evenings and came back late, but she had forbidden herself to ask him any more personal questions.

"An old college friend is living in Georgetown now," Race answered easily.

"Male or female?" Vicky heard her voice ask, and could have slugged herself.

Race's eyes danced. "Why, Victoria, are you actually showing an interest in my private life?"

"No," she grumbled. "What are we having to eat?"

The meal was cold in deference to the heat of the day. They enjoyed a few beers and pleasant conversation. Vicky had always assumed Race had inherited his charm and easy ways from Hank, but now it occurred to her he might have learned them from Wade. The man was warm, friendly, easy to talk to and an attentive listener. He was also here, she guessed, to look into landscaping possibilities in accordance with Race's plans for Oak Hill. And Vicky was determined to disappoint them both.

After lunch she adamantly refused to help Race do the dishes, pointing out that he had never helped her to wash the one-to-two-hundred food pans used daily at the kennel. She wandered out onto the veranda with Wade. They chatted companionably for a while, mostly about the property.

"It sure is a beautiful place," Wade said admiringly, looking down toward the river.

"Yes. I can't imagine why you and Race want to fill it up with buildings," she said bluntly.

"Well, now, Vicky, I can see your point and even agree with it to a certain extent. It's lovely and peaceful the way it is, and private, too. On the other hand, I know what possibilities Race sees in it, and that has its merits, too. As a landscaper, I look out on this overgrown land and see a lot of potential going to waste."

"Yes, it's overgrown around here. It could do with some more work. But the thought of looking out there one day and seeing ticky-tacky suburban houses with polished lawns is more than I can bear."

Wade looked surprised. "Is that really what you think he wants to do to this place?"

"Sure. Isn't it?"

"Vicky, hasn't he shown you any of his work?"

"No." She paused, then admitted honestly, "I've never asked him about his work."

Wade looked thoroughly disgusted for a moment. "Do the two of you ever talk like sensible adults? Or do you just spend all your time going for each other's throats?"

"I guess we do argue a lot," admitted Vicky sheepishly.

Wade took her arm and drew her inside, into a sunny room. It had once been the dining room, but Race had turned it into a makeshift office. His drafting board was set up near a window. He'd clearly been working on something recently, as the board was covered with notes and sketches. The room was dominated by a large, old table covered with drawings, plans, papers, notes, pens, pencils, rulers, tools, implements and coffee cups.

"Now where's he put them?" muttered Wade. "Ah, there they are."

A stack of leather-bound portfolios sat on a chair in the far corner. Wade picked them up, brought them to the table and opened the first one.

"These are drawings and photographs of his past projects," Wade explained. "These here are buildings he designed or helped design when he used to work for a big firm in California."

Vicky looked through the first few portfolios without much interest. His work in those days had comprised office buildings, factories, shops, restaurants, hotels and a few homes. They were attractive, progressive buildings, certainly something he could take pride in, but she didn't relish the thought of any of them standing on her property.

"Now these," said Wade as he opened the remaining portfolios, "are his real work. He started taking private commissions about seven years ago. Then when he was thirty, he cut loose and quit his job. Said he'd never build another thing he didn't want to build. Of course, even Race has to compromise now and then."

The difference was stunning. Each building was entirely unique and special in itself, absorbed into the landscape with total harmony and balance. Whatever the setting, each structure looked as if it had been born into the scene rather than placed there arbitrarily. And although each building was different from every other one, Race's style was stamped on each one even for Vicky's untrained eye to see: strong, elegant, daring—and even outrageous on one or two occasions.

His independent work, Vicky noted, consisted primarily of private homes, although there was one private stable and one small church. The church was extraordinary; sitting on the edge of a seaside cliff, it seemed to soar out into space and reach up to the sky.

"That's incredible," Vicky breathed.

"What are you doing?" asked Race, coming in from the kitchen.

"Doing what you should have done weeks ago—showing Vicky some of your work," scolded Wade.

"She never asked to see it."

"Well, why didn't you tell me you did things like this?" she chided him. "For goodness' sake, Race, when you said luxury homes, I thought you meant something like those hideous things on the far side of the main highway."

"Vicky!" He was insulted.

"Don't look so shocked," she said, laughing.

"How would you feel if I said I thought you ran a flea-ridden dump and starved all your boarders?"

"I get your point. But how was I to know? These are incredible, Race!" She looked at him with deliberate condescension. "I guess there's more to you than meets the eye."

There was a wicked look in his eyes, reminding her suddenly of some of the other unexpected qualities she'd discovered in him. But since Wade was chaperoning them, he said only, "I'm glad you should think so, Vicky."

She sneered at him and went back to studying the photographs and drawings.

"It seems like you guys get a lot of work," she remarked.

"We get enough," said Race.

"So why is it, if you're doing so well out there in California, you want to come and build here?"

"A lot of reasons. Mostly because I suddenly found myself the owner—"

"*Co*-owner."

"Co-owner," he amended with a grin, "of some beautiful land near a big city with a wealthy population. It's a different climate and a different region from the ones I've been working in, so it would be a new challenge. And mostly I was hoping that since I already own the land anyhow, I could take my time and do exactly what I want to do without compromising."

Vicky's eyes held his for a quiet moment as she absorbed the full impact of his words. She turned away from his strong, steady gaze to leaf through more photographs, but her mind was elsewhere and her heart was sinking.

As long as she had believed mere greed and impatience were what motivated him, she could feel resentful and self-righteous. But something in his words and his eyes told her that he wanted Oak Hill every bit as badly as she did, and for the same reasons: to fulfill an important ambition to do a job that mattered to him and to do it as well as it could be done. And looking at the evidence of his enormous talent, she knew she had no right to cheat him out of his opportunity if she couldn't make Oak Hill the best of kennels. She suddenly felt tired and depressed.

"Thank you for showing these to me," she said softly. "I have to go—get back to work now."

She exchanged quick farewells with the two men and walked to the kennel pensively. There was no way they could both win. And whoever lost would lose more than a few acres of land.

July the Fourth turned out to be an overwhelming success for Vicky and for the kennel. They had a full house; they did their biggest grooming business ever; they were interviewed by a local TV station and by the *Washington Post* and they were promised a lot of return business. Vicky worked sixteen hours a day for four solid days. Her presence wasn't actually needed all of that time, but the holiday was a major turning point for the kennel and she would have cheerfully given her right arm to make sure everything went well.

The most surprising thing was that absolutely nothing went wrong. It all ran like clockwork. Given that it was the busiest four days they'd ever had and that the nature of the business was a vast number of live, unpredictable animals always capable of providing the unexpected and inexplicable, Vicky was astonished and overwhelmingly relieved that it had all come off without a hitch. She had, of course, prepared for every eventuality and carefully instructed her staff. But she had still firmly expected something unforeseeable to happen and was enormously gratified that it hadn't. She took it as a good omen for the future of the kennel.

Joe Hanley, the obedience instructor, had invited Wade and Race to join his family for a Fourth of July picnic. She'd been right in her assumption that Joe and Wade would hit it off. Within five minutes of their introduction to each other by Vicky, they'd discovered they both had a passion for baseball and a fascination with vintage cars. Race had rolled his eyes when he'd heard them conferring enthusiastically and had told Vicky she didn't know what she had started. She knew that after the picnic at Joe's, Race and Wade had gone to join friends in the city to watch fireworks on the Mall.

Vicky had spent all of the holiday hard at work looking after more than 250 animals. After a weary Independence Day toast with her staff, she'd spent most of the night at the kennel as well, going around in the dark to comfort trembling nervous dogs frightened by the sound of fireworks in the distance.

But now the holiday was over and she'd returned to a more normal working schedule. She walked to the outdoor aisle of one of the wings and hooked up her high-pressure hose. She wore her usual costume. The sun was high in the sky; the day was oppressively hot and humid. Most of the dogs were inside, taking advantage of the shadowed interiors and cooling fans. Vicky and the staff went outside every hour to hose down, to keep the exteriors as clean and cool as possible.

Vicky was absorbed in this task when a cascade of icy cold water hit her from behind. She whirled around to see Nadine put down one empty bucket and pick up another full one, getting ready to throw it at her. Vicky held up her hose like a gun and hit Nadine with a strong blast of freezing cold water. Nadine shrieked, hit Vicky square in the face with the second bucket of water and ran around the corner, laughing.

Well, why not? thought Vicky. They needed a release from the tension and hard work of the past week. With a shrug and a wicked grin, she unhooked her hose and ran around the corner with it. Another of Oak Hill's infamous water fights had begun.

She turned the corner to the second aisle and was hit by three buckets of water at once. She sputtered, shook her hair out of her face and opened her eyes to see Nadine, Rebecca and Désirée all laughing gleefully.

"You're all fired!" shrieked Vicky, and machine-gunned them with her hose. They all laughed even harder at her bemused expression when no water came out; she hadn't re-connected it to the water line yet.

She dropped the hose and went for Nadine, the smallest, and dragged her forcibly under one of the overhead faucets.

"No fair! No fair!" screamed Nadine.

"I don't have to be fair. I'm the boss," Vicky pointed out, and soaked Nadine from head to foot.

Vicky wrestled a hose away from Rebecca and went off to stake out her own territory. A Newfoundland, a water dog by breeding, wanted to get into the act, so Vicky obligingly sprayed him down and let him chase the swift stream of water around his run for a few minutes while she lay in wait for the others.

She heard a movement behind her and whirled swiftly, spraying the intruder from head to foot with a deft flick of her wrist before she recognized him.

"Race!"

The look on his dripping face was one of comical disbelief, followed by one of excessive patience with a naughty child.

"Hi, Vicky. Would you mind turning that off, please?"

"What? Oh. Sorry." She realized she was still spraying him and released her pressure on the nozzle. She moved toward him, her hand pressed against her mouth in an unsuccessful attempt to stifle her laughter. She knew her mirthful apology sounded distinctly insincere. He had been rather nicely dressed, too.

She saw the deviltry in his eyes too late. In another second he had grabbed her with one strong arm and turned her own hose on her with his free hand.

"No, Race! Race, no!" She shrieked with cold and laughter as the chilling water jetted over her bare stomach and long legs.

Rebecca rounded the corner, armed for revenge, and got a clear shot at them both with her hose. Then they were all hit from overhead by Désirée, who had climbed up onto the roof with her hose. Rebecca and Vicky turned their hoses on

Désirée, who prudently retreated down the other side of the sloping roof.

Vicky dealt summarily with Rebecca and then, determined to get even, dashed off after Race, who had disappeared round another corner. As she ran past an open doorway, Race stepped out and hit her with a bucketful of water. He ran off with her hose while she sputtered in outrage, "You sneak! Hiding behind doors!"

Twenty minutes and a considerable quantity of water later, Vicky was the victor of the game, having acquired two hoses and having managed to trap the three women in a dead end from her vantage point on the roof. Race spoiled the effect by sneaking up behind her and dumping a bucket of water over her head while the others were crying uncle; how he managed to climb onto the roof while carrying a bucket of water, she never did figure out.

They all cheerfully raided Nadine's grooming room for a supply of towels and went to the lounge to dry off, laughing and teasing one another.

"You realize we've got to go back out there in twenty minutes to hose down again, don't you?" Vicky reminded the women.

They all groaned and Rebecca flopped to the floor in a melodramatic swoon. Brian came into the room to talk to Vicky, but it was rather hopeless. Brian was normally feebleminded around Désirée anyhow, but the sight of her glistening from head to toe while her skimpy costume clung to her like a second skin seemed to rob him of all power of speech. Vicky finally sent him away with orders not to return until he could remember what he wanted to ask her.

She was exceedingly glad that Race did no more than glance briefly at Désirée with mild appreciation. She told herself she felt that way only because she didn't want to see every male around go deaf and dumb at the sight of the girl.

The uproar died down and the three women gradually went back to remembered chores. Vicky eyed Race with amusement.

"You learned the game fast," she teased him.

"The rules are pretty simple: dog eat dog."

Vicky groaned. "Did you just come here to saturate me and make bad puns?"

"No. Actually I came over to ask you out."

She looked at him suspiciously.

He grinned knowingly. "Properly chaperoned, of course. It's Wade's last night in town, and seeing as you didn't get any real Fourth of July, we thought we'd take you to the carnival that's in town."

"A carnival? I've never been to a carnival."

"You've never been to a carnival?"

"No one's ever taken me," she explained. Not her father; not the men she'd dated; not the kids she knew at school.

Race seemed to sense he'd inadvertently touched a sore spot and didn't press the point. "Well, then, that settles it. You, of all people, will love a carnival. Be ready at eight o'clock, okay?"

"Okay," she said almost shyly.

He started to leave. "Oh, Vicky?"

"Yes?"

His eyes raked her. "Much as I like your outfit, could you wear something different tonight? I don't want to have to help you beat off half the men in the county."

Vicky stood dizzily in the middle of the fairground and tried to get her bearings. She had made Race take her on the Tilt-A-Whirl three times in a row, and now she regretted it. Race feebly leaned against a tree trunk. Wade, who had sat out the last round, chuckled at them both.

"How could I have let you talk me into that?" groaned Race.

"Oh, but it's so much fun!" insisted Vicky. She tried to walk toward him but found she had taken a step backward instead. She stopped in confusion.

Wade guided them both to a bench, where she and Race sat, head in hands, for ten minutes.

"I'm hungry," Vicky announced at last.

"How can you possibly be hungry after that?" demanded Race.

"I worked all day and I didn't have any dinner," she pointed out. "You guys invited me out; feed me."

And they did: she devoured a candied apple, a foot-long hot dog, roasted peanuts, two beers, a cola, an ice-cream sandwich and, at Wade's insistence, a cotton candy.

"It's so pretty!" she exclaimed. She made Race buy her a second one, since it wasn't very filling after all.

"Do you always eat this much?" he asked warily.

"Not always. But I told you I've never been to a carnival before. I want to try everything!"

Determined to please, Vicky's escorts took her on a dozen more rides. They offered to try to win her a stuffed animal or two at one of the games booths, but she pointed out that she already had more live animals than she knew what to do with and had no use for a stuffed one. They watched people throwing balls at a target in order to dunk a woman in water; Vicky found it dull in comparison to water fights at Oak Hill. In the Fun House she looked at her short, squat image in a curved mirror and decided not to ask for another hot dog.

The flashy colored lights, the gay music, the whirling, whizzing rides and the whole festival atmosphere thrilled Vicky. She loved every minute of it and enjoyed capturing a lost bit of childhood.

"I didn't know what I was missing all those years." She laughed, playing with a glow-in-the-dark balloon Wade had just bought her. She caught Race's gaze on her, dark gray and unreadable. Wade gave her a friendly squeeze.

"Oh, look! I want to go on that! We haven't done that yet!" she exclaimed, her eyes wide.

"The Ferris wheel?" Wade asked. They all looked at the tall, brightly lit wheel spinning around gracefully high above the ground.

"Yes! Come on, you two!"

Wade shook his head ruefully. "Sorry, Vicky. I've got a thing about heights."

"Race?"

"Okay, but I have a feeling I'll regret this."

"Don't be silly. It looks wonderful," she said enthusiastically.

It was, in fact, wonderful. Vicky experienced a peculiar dropping sensation in her stomach every time they descended from the top of the Ferris wheel's arc to the bottom, but the soaring sensation on the way up was so exciting, the view of the local town and countryside so beautiful at night, that she didn't mind. They were very near the top when the Ferris wheel stopped moving.

"What's happening?" she asked.

"They're just taking someone off and putting someone else on."

"I didn't realize it was this high," she said uncomfortably as she looked down. The ground seemed very far away.

"Look out over the valley," Race said, pointing to the distance to distract her.

The Ferris wheel jerked briefly into motion, then stopped again when Vicky and Race were at the very top of the wheel. The pause seemed to take longer this time. To keep herself from looking down, she looked at Race. He was looking at her with that dark, unreadable expression again.

"What's wrong?" she asked artlessly.

"Nothing." He smiled and his brooding look was gone.

"They're taking an awfully long time down there," she said nervously. "Could something be broken?"

"I doubt it," answered Race, trying unsuccessfully to see what was happening far below them. Their seat rocked slightly when he moved. Vicky gasped.

Race looked at her tense expression and smiled. "Don't worry. It won't be anything serious."

"What if we're stuck up here?"

"Stop imagining the worst, Vicky. Probably someone's just gotten locked into their seat or dropped a contact lens or something," he said reassuringly.

Vicky edged a little closer to his warmth and didn't look down again. Race took her hand in his and squeezed it. The sky behind them was black and full of stars. The moonlight cast a tarnished halo in his brown hair, as if he became a wicked fallen angel at night. His smoky gray gaze held a tender light as it moved over her face and hair. One corner of his mouth lifted in that half smile he had whenever a private thought amused him.

"When I was a teenager," he said slowly, "we used to try to take our minds off it whenever this happened."

The Ferris wheel jerked slightly but didn't move forward. She clutched Race's hand. "How?" she asked breathlessly.

"Like this," he whispered.

Slowly, ever so slowly, he lowered his mouth to hers. Vicky held as still as a wild animal when his warm, firm lips touched her soft ones. Her eyelids fluttered down as his lips tenderly, gently, pliantly teased hers, tasting, coaxing, caressing. She finally moved slightly in response, answering his sweet kisses.

"You taste like cotton candy," he murmured against her lips. She could hear the amusement in his voice mingled with the heady, restrained passion that was leaping between them.

Race's strong arm pulled her a little closer as his other hand gently caressed her waist and stomach. Their kisses deepened, but still his touch was soft and gentle, like a shy boy courting his first sweetheart. Their tongues touched lightly, then stayed to explore each other slowly. His mouth tasted sweet and warm to Vicky. She felt as if she were drowning in honey.

A liquid fire started in her belly and spread throughout her body. She had indeed forgotten about being stuck high above the ground on her first Ferris wheel ride ever. She knew only the warm breeze touching her like a lover, the hard feel of Race's body, his warm lips and his satiny smooth tongue sliding into her mouth as it teased and tickled and caressed hers. She caught his tongue gently between her teeth and tugged on it teasingly. A low moan escaped him, filling her with an unbearable excitement....

The Ferris wheel came to life with another jerk. Vicky clutched Race roughly and bit his lip. He grunted in surprise and pulled away from her with a martyred look. She pushed herself away from him to grip the safety bar. She gasped as they descended swiftly to the ground and then rose again, her hair flying behind her.

Two more swift rotations, then Vicky and Race were the ones getting off while others waited at the top. She shyly avoided Race's knowing eyes and teasing smile and went to find Wade in the crowd. He was watching a snake dancer and could only be dragged away when Vicky insisted he take her to get her palm read.

"What a load of rubbish," she said afterward. "Success in love; success in business; a long and happy life."

"Were you hoping for something different?" Wade asked, chuckling.

"She could have at least been a little more creative," Vicky complained. "You know. Beware of one-eyed toothless men; you will soon meet a stranger with a valuable secret; don't swim without a lucky charm. That sort of thing."

She ate a box of popcorn, then insisted on one last ride on the Tilt-A-Whirl before they left. It was a mistake.

"I don't feel so good," she mumbled as they walked to Race's car. In deference to Race's request that day, she was wearing a modest sea-green blouse and her newest pair of jeans. The jeans were still rather tight, and she was regretting everything: her choice of pants, her appetite and her enthusiasm for the Tilt-A-Whirl.

"What's wrong?" asked Wade.

"I would guess she's got a stomachache," said Race dryly.

She collapsed in the back seat of the car and closed her eyes. They'd been on the road for only five minutes when she said in a peculiar voice, "Pull over, Race."

She ran into the dark woods at the side of the road. When she came back to the car, she looked haggard and exhausted.

"If you say a damned thing—" she warned Race.

"Who, me?" he replied with wide-eyed innocence.

She rode with her head out the window the rest of the way home, just in case.

When they parked in the driveway at the manor house, Wade advised Race to see her home safely.

"I've walked that path at night a hundred times," she argued sleepily.

"In your current condition you're liable to walk into a tree or fall off the bridge," Race said insultingly.

Actually, she was grateful for the firm hand on her elbow as she negotiated the bumpy path down to the river. In her nauseated and dizzy condition, she would have landed on her face once or twice if he hadn't been there to steady her.

"You're enjoying this," she accused him.

"It's been a lovely evening," he said, deliberately misunderstanding her.

"It has been," she agreed contritely as they crossed the river. "Thanks for taking me, Race. I guess it's about the best date I've ever had."

The hand on her arm stilled her, and Race swung her around to look searchingly into her eyes. He opened his mouth to speak when suddenly the peace of the night was shattered by Rebel's barked greeting. The ducks woke up and quacked in surprise and irritation, attracting her attention. Rebel came racing down to the river, ran straight past Vicky and Race and hurled her furry dark body into the water. The ducks quacked loudly in indignation. A few of them flew away, but most of them just paddled upstream while Rebel swam after them, barking merrily.

"What the—?"

"Rebel!" Vicky shouted, adding to the noise level. "Rebel! come back here! I've told you not to chase the ducks! Rebel!"

Rebel ignored her. It was with some difficulty that Race restrained Vicky from jumping into the dark river after her dog. In the distance, the sleeping dogs in the kennel heard

the noise and started barking as well. The still country night
had turned to pandemonium in a matter of moments.

"I had remembered it as such a peaceful place," said
Race wryly.

It took several minutes to convince Rebel to come out of
the water. Vicky castigated her noisily all the way home, to
a fading chorus of quacks and barks. Race followed them
into the cottage. He looked questioningly at Vicky as she
turned on the kitchen lights and opened the refrigerator.

"I have to feed her," she explained. "Would you please
get a towel from the bathroom? She's soaking wet."

Race returned with the towel to find Vicky looking pale
as she mixed Rebel's food.

"I'll do that," he offered. "Why don't you go get ready
for bed?"

Vicky complied gratefully and went to wash up, brush her
teeth, comb her hair and change into her short cotton bathrobe.

She went back out to find the situation under control.
Rebel was only mildly damp and eagerly waiting for Race to
finish mixing her supper. After he put her food down for
her, he looked consideringly around the main room of the
cottage. The walls and floors were wooden, and Vicky had
decorated in a simple rustic style. Her military upbringing
had taught her to keep a tidy house. It came to her suddenly that this had once been Race's home.

"Does it seem at all familiar?" she asked.

"Yes, it does. I like what you've done with it. That door
frame is falling apart, though. I'll fix it for you this week."

"You don't need to do that."

"I don't mind." He looked at her, his gaze sliding down
to her bathrobe and her long bare legs. She always slept in
the nude, and she suddenly felt acutely aware of her naked
body beneath the thin cotton robe. As if he'd followed her
thoughts, he grinned and said, "I'd better say good-night
now."

He came forward and without warning kissed her gently, slowly on the mouth. He pulled back to look into her face and frowned.

"Are you okay? You look funny," he said.

"I don't know. How do girls usually look when you kiss them?"

"They don't usually turn green."

"No, I—I don't feel . . . I'm going to . . . Let yourself out, will you, Race?" She turned and fled for the bathroom.

Ten minutes later, in her dark, peaceful cottage, she fell into bed, vowing never to eat, drink, ride the Tilt-A-Whirl or kiss Race Bennett ever again.

Six

Vicky woke up the next morning with a mild headache but otherwise felt no worse for the wear. She immediately violated two of last night's vows by eating a bowl of cereal and drinking half a pitcher of orange juice. Once fortified by breakfast, she decided she could even be tempted back on the Tilt-A-Whirl someday.

As for Race... The remembered pleasure of his touch, the slow delight of his kisses, burned in her mind, weakening her resolve. It was extraordinary that a man so strong and so powerful could be so gentle and so tender. No one had ever touched Vicky like that before. He was like a sorcerer, hypnotizing her, invading her thoughts, unlocking dark secrets and hidden needs in her. She closed her eyes and shuddered slightly. She felt a deep yearning, an actual physical ache. And for what? For the touch of a man she was constantly at odds with? She had been right when she'd told him any involvement between them would be a mistake under the circumstances. But good sense couldn't change the way she felt or what she wanted.

She was pensive and distracted at work that morning, her heart at war with her head. She was glad Race had taken Wade to the airport, after a brief but friendly goodbye at the kennel, and then gone into town to run errands; she didn't want to face him alone until the memory of last night had faded a bit. He had a way of throwing her off balance, and she couldn't afford that.

In the end, it was a mere phone call that caused her to remember the previous night with perturbation instead of longing.

"Good morning, Oak Hill Pet Motel," she said as she answered the phone.

"Hello. I'm calling from California. Is Race Bennett available, by any chance?" It was a young woman's voice, hollow and far away.

"No, he's gone to town. You'd best try him at home, though. The number is—"

"I've got the number. But there's never any answer, and he hasn't called me for a few days. Can I leave a message with you?"

"All right," said Vicky with a noticeable lack of enthusiasm.

"Just tell him to call Karen."

"Last name? Phone number?"

"He'll know. That's Karen, okay?"

"Okay."

Vicky hung up the phone and stared at it with a slight frown. What a fool she was! A woman in California calling for Race. Lately it had completely slipped her mind that he had an entire life back there: a home, a business, friends, favorite haunts—and women. Yes, Race would definitely have a woman out there, maybe more than one. He was intelligent, charming, attractive, successful and, as Vicky was discovering to her discomfort, charged with a magnetic, masculine sex appeal. Of course there were women! And he was probably bored with his dull life out here in the country, repairing an old house and playing an occasional game of cards with Joe Hanley; so, now and again when the mood took him, he livened things up by dallying with an over-tall, freckle-faced, muscular kennel girl. And she had responded by mooning over him like some naive, half-witted, lovesick country bumpkin hankering after a movie star!

"Oh," Vicky said viciously. "Well, he can go jump in the river if he thinks that's the way it's going to be!" Perhaps he even thought he could use his virility to ensure her cooperation when he started bulldozing the kennel! She muttered a lot of bad words—foul, nasty expressions she had picked up from sailors in her youth.

She had worked herself up into a fine self-righteous rage by the time Race appeared that afternoon. The warm light in his eyes quickly changed to astonishment as she gave him the message from Karen, tartly informed him she was not his answering service and then rudely told him to get out from underfoot, since she had a lot of work to do and no time to waste answering stupid questions from someone who couldn't even tell the difference between a Lhasa Apso and a Maltese.

"What have I done now?" he demanded.

"I told you to keep your hands off me!" she hurled at him.

His eyebrows shot up in surprise. "Is this all about last night? Oh, come on, Vicky. If you didn't want me to touch you, all you had to do was—"

"Of all the cheap tricks," she accused him, not wanting to be reminded of her enthusiastic participation in their embrace, "making moves on a girl at the top of a Ferris wheel!"

"Cheap trick? You seemed pretty impressed by it at the time," Race shot back.

Her cheeks reddened as she realized he would of course know that she had enjoyed it. He would remember the way she held him, returned his kisses, drew his tongue into her mouth....

Race saw her confusion and pressed his advantage. He grabbed her shoulders and forced her to meet his eyes.

"I'm not a clumsy schoolboy, Vicky," he said impatiently. "I know when a woman enjoys me." He narrowed his eyes as a sudden suspicion dawned. "Is this all because Karen phoned from California? If you're worried about her—"

It was probably the worst thing he could have said under the circumstances, had he but known it. Vicky went pale and wrenched away from him.

"I can't throw you off my land, but I want you to stay away from me," she said in a low, furious voice.

Race stared at her for a long moment, anger and puzzled concern warring in his expression. For a second she feared he would attempt to prove to her there and then how well he knew her desires, and she wasn't sure how her traitorous body would react. But in the end, anger won out.

"Stay away from you? I'd rather wrestle with a Mojave rattlesnake than come near you again, Miss Wood," he snapped, and stormed out of the kennel.

True to his word, Race avoided Vicky as if she had the bubonic plague. He spoke to her only when absolutely necessary, and then only at the kennel, in the presence of others. He threw himself into his private projects with renewed vigor, and she could hear him hammering and sawing with a vengeance when she went down to the river in the hot, still afternoons; for despite her promise, Vicky still swam naked when she thought he was otherwise occupied. The heat and humidity were intense, and she couldn't resist the clear, cool water. It wasn't until Saturday evening that she had a moment alone with him. And that was by accident.

In a way, evenings were her favorite time at the kennel. The office was closed; the phone was hooked into the answering machine; there were no customers and the chaotic grooming room was empty. The intense heat of the afternoon lifted, so work wasn't as taxing. And since the heaviest chores were done during the day, it was a fairly easy shift. The setting sun cast a soft golden light through the windows and the dogs started to settle down for the night, giving the whole kennel a relaxed atmosphere. Usually only one or two people worked this shift. Vicky always worked Saturday night so that only one staff member a week had to sacrifice date-night-America to duty. Tonight Brian was with her, grumbling and groaning melodramatically about what he was missing because he was stuck here with Vicky, who always insisted she was too old for him.

"But if you'd grow a beard I might change my mind," Vicky teased him. At eighteen, Brian was a well-developed lad, but he still couldn't grow more on his face than an unimpressive peach fuzz, much to his chagrin. Brian sighed like a martyr and started washing the floors. Vicky collected dirty towels and rugs and took them to the grooming room to throw into the washing machine.

Arms filled to overflowing with dirty laundry, Vicky kicked open the door and walked into the grooming room—and stopped dead in her tracks.

Race was using the big shower, which, originally designed for dogs, had no door or curtain. Water jetted down on his naked body, making it shine and gleam like oiled bronze. His wet hair was dark, showing no trace of his golden halo. He turned quickly at her noisy entrance.

They both stood as still as startled deer. Vicky tightened her arms on the laundry as if it would escape from her. Water beat down on Race. Their eyes held as they stood immobile, transfixed. The world faded out, and Vicky knew only those smoky gray eyes in that dark visage. His expression was unreadable, enigmatic; he seemed a stranger, a dark glistening river god caught bathing by a mere mortal. Vicky took a deep convulsive breath. With a compelling curiosity she couldn't control and a fear she didn't understand, she let her gaze drift down his body.

He was long and lean and perfectly proportioned, from his broad, tanned shoulders down to his narrow hips, where the flesh was paler, all the way down the length of his powerful legs. Dark gold hair glistened on his arms and chest and legs, bleached by a winter sun. Her eyes were drawn to the darker hair at his lower torso, and she felt a primitive hunger grip her. Her gaze traveled swiftly back up his hard belly and across his smoothly muscled chest. He stood before her, proudly masculine, natural and unashamed. Vicky's eyes met his again, and she wondered if he could see in them the turmoil that was rushing through her.

He studied her face for a tense moment, and then he broke into a broad, boyish grin; from Lucifer to a leprechaun in the wink of an eye, she mused.

"Join me?" he invited teasingly, and held out a hand.

"I wouldn't dream of disturbing you."

"Have I disturbed you?" he asked knowingly.

Vicky dropped dirty laundry all over the floor. "As long as you're using my shower—"

"It's Nadine's shower, and she said I could—"

"You can make yourself useful. Before you go, stick all this in the washing machine and turn it on."

"Have I ever refused you anything, partner?"

Vicky stalked out of the room with as much dignity as she could muster.

Not long after, Race came into the kitchen, where Brian was holding a nervous poodle while Vicky prepared a hypodermic injection.

"What are you doing?" Race asked.

"Insulin injection," she explained. "He's a diabetic."

Race was dressed in pale trousers and an apricot shirt that complimented his dark golden looks. His hair was still damp, and a fresh, clean scent clung to him. As soon as Vicky met his eyes, his look impertinently reminded her that he knew she had admired and been affected by what lay under his clothes.

"Hot date tonight, Race?" asked Brian enviously. He didn't wait for an answer. "You see, Vicky? Everyone is painting the town red tonight except us!"

"Brian, once a month won't kill you. You can meditate on your many sins while you do the last hosing outside," she admonished him.

"And you, Vicky?" asked Race.

"Oh, her," Brian said with disgust. "Wasting her youth and good looks. Spends every Saturday night washing towels and dishing out heartworm pills."

"Not because I don't have anything better to do on a Saturday night," she added frostily.

"All part of being the boss?" Race asked without mockery.

"That's right. All right, Brian, let's have a look at him."

The little dog squirmed nervously in Brian's arms, but Vicky had the touch. She calmed and soothed the little dog with her gentle, confident hands and, once certain he trusted her, injected him quickly and efficiently so that he scarcely felt it. In fact, he licked her face when it was over. She looked up to find Race watching her intently.

"You really chose the right line of work," he said softly.

"I told you I do better with animals than with people," she replied simply. There was a long, uneasy pause. "Hadn't you better be going?"

"Yes," he answered. "Don't work too late."

"Hear that, Vicky?" said Brian hopefully.

She watched Race go—to meet a woman? She felt unreasonably resentful, as if it were he and not Brian who belonged with her here tonight. She thought of him with another women, talking, laughing, enjoying her company, enjoying her body—

"I'll do the last hosing by myself, Brian," she said suddenly. "I could use the exercise. Why don't you leave early?"

The airline strike was an unexpected and highly expensive event for Vicky. She felt as if they'd gone on strike to inconvenience her personally. Why not last year? Why not next year? Why *now*, for God's sake? she wondered. Thousands of people were forced to cancel business trips and vacations. And too many of them were Vicky's customers. Cancellations came in by the dozen at Oak Hill. It was a big setback. July had promised to be such a good month; she had counted on banking quite a bit of cash. The strike had taken a huge bite out of Oak Hill's income, and the kennel's fate swung in the balance.

On the other hand, the strike couldn't last long. A week at the most? All those business trips could take place then. Some of the vacations would be postponed till Christmas or next summer, but other people would take off as soon as a settlement was reached and the planes were in the air again. Only then would Vicky know how much she could recover her losses.

Why now? she wondered for the hundredth time as she pushed food around on her plate....

"Vicky?" said an anxious male voice.

She looked up at Dean Alexander, the vet, across the dinner table, guiltily aware that she'd been drifting away and ignoring him again. He knew the whole situation and had been sympathetic. Extremely understanding as well, considering that he was buying her dinner at the most expensive restaurant in the area and all evening she had been about as attentive as a tree stump.

"Sorry, Dean. Drifting again."

"Oh, I thought you might not like the food. You usually have such a good appetite."

"Race says I eat as much as a whole construction crew," she said dryly.

"But then you do enough work for a whole construction crew," said Dean admiringly. "I don't know how you do it."

"I was built for hard work."

"And for other things. You're a beautiful woman, Vicky."

"Thank you," she mumbled, slightly embarrassed. Dean was a nice guy and his compliment had been sincere, but Vicky was on thin ice here. This was exactly the sort of thing she had always hated, could never enjoy, could never handle well: a romantic candlelight dinner, polite conversation and flattering comments, which she lacked the social skills to either accept gracefully or return in kind. Only this was worse. Now a man she liked personally and respected

professionally was looking at her with an open fascination
she couldn't return; far from finding it flattering, she found
it a burden. She had no idea how to kindly make known her
complete lack of sexual interest in him. She had even less of
an idea why she suddenly found his attentions so tiresome
when only a few weeks ago she had considered encouraging
them. He was, after all, a kind, intelligent, attractive man
who had many things in common with her.

Vicky shifted uncomfortably. She had dressed carefully
for the evening, since she had so few opportunities to wear
pretty clothes; but now she felt almost naked without her
shorts, T-shirt and ponytail. She wore a simple pale green
silk dress that had a tight bodice with thin shoulder straps
and a full skirt. Her gleaming red hair was newly washed
and sweet smelling, pulled back from her face by two deli-
cately enameled clips, and fell around her shoulders in silky
abundance. She wore no jewelry and very little makeup,
since she was not particularly confident in her skill at ap-
plying it. Her shoes, of course, were flat so she wouldn't
tower over her date. Vicky, in any event, found wearing high
heels riskier than trying to capture a vicious German shepherd.

Race occasionally complained that she always said exactly what she thought, no matter how inappropriate or
cutting it might be. She wondered briefly what he would say
if he could see her now, murmuring awkward polite responses and pretending great interest in her meal to avoid
further conversation.

Race... She wondered uneasily if this strike would swing
things in his favor.

"More wine, Vicky?"

"Yes, please."

Draining the glass kept her busy and gave her a pleasantly remote feeling. Why hadn't she ever realized before
that the only things she could discuss easily with Dean were
dogs and health? All other subjects made her feel awkward
or naive in the man's presence; it was the story of her life.
The only men she could talk to about anything and every-

thing were always men with whom any sexual relationship was never a possibility: Hank, Joe Hanley, Brian, Race.... Race?

Dean was addressing some comment to her. She tried to look interested. Poor guy; he would do so much better with any of the interested women who looked his way whenever he took Vicky out. She was pondering his potential for happiness with other women when someone came by their table to rescue her for a few minutes. It was a local woman who owned a menagerie of pets that required Dean's and Vicky's various services. Vicky liked her.

"I met your new partner the other day, Vicky," she said. "I remember his mother from—oh, it must be over twenty years ago. Shame about her death. Kate Bennett was a fine woman. Her son certainly inherited her good looks. Doesn't look a bit like Hank, does he?"

"You knew?"

"Sure. Everybody around here knew. And now that the boy is back, I reckon them what knows will tell them that doesn't. That's how these things spread. But then, Race doesn't seem to want to hide it any more than he wants to talk about it."

"Where did you meet him?" asked Vicky.

"Town Hall."

An uneasy feeling crept through Vicky's wine-induced fog. "Town Hall? What was he doing there?"

"He seemed to be checking into zoning laws, building codes, property taxes, all that sort of thing. He's an architect, isn't he? Seems he's going to build around here."

"He *thinks* he's going to build around here," Vicky muttered. After that she missed the rest of the conversation, which touched on a recent scandal at the local mortuary.

So Race thought she had lost already, did he, that the kennel was washed up? He certainly hadn't wasted any time in setting about making preparations to bulldoze her life, the filthy, scheming hyena. Hot rage seethed inside her. The next time she saw him, she would tell him in graphic detail what he could do with his plans.

She was distracted and monosyllabic through the rest of the evening, but she was able to spare Dean some pity for being out with such a glum, foul-tempered dullard. The wine didn't loosen her tongue, but it fed her temper. She imbibed steadily, only half listening to Dean as she planned all the inappropriate and cutting things she would say to Race the next time he waltzed into the kennel as if he owned it.

The air had been heavy and still all day as the atmospheric pressure decreased. Now, as Vicky and Dean stepped out of the restaurant, the night was wild with wind and the sky was brewing a violent, spinning storm. She tried to pretend regret as she asked to be taken home immediately. Dean was, for reasons quite beyond her, genuinely reluctant to end the evening but told her he could see the wisdom of her request.

As they drove, the rain began hitting the windshield in fat, heavy drops. Dean pulled into the driveway in front of Race's house, since the walk to Vicky's cottage was shorter from there. The storm was violent and heavy by now, and the rain poured so thickly she could barely see out the car window to the house.

"Thanks for a lovely evening, Dean." She used the stock phrase, and it sounded as awful as she had feared.

His hand on her arm stilled her. "Don't go out in that stuff, Vicky. Wait till it clears up a bit."

With an uncomfortable smile, she agreed. Tearing through the woods in the pelting rain easily seemed preferable to sitting in the closed, dark car and trying to think of something to say. She glanced out the window and peered through the torrential downpour, trying to see the house. It looked dark. Did that mean the electric lines had fallen? Or was Race off on another date, dallying with more wide-eyed country girls, practicing his smooth moves on them? Vicky felt as if someone had stabbed her and twisted the knife. Damn him! Damn him for coming to the only home she'd ever had and trying to take it away from her, for disrupting her life and peace of mind, for seducing her senses as the serpent seduced Eve, for making her jealous of him when she had to keep refusing him herself. Rather dog in the manger of her, that last one, she thought. Now she was making bad puns, too. Damn him! She threw her head back and closed her eyes.

"Vicky..."

She looked up. Dean was watching her very seriously. She suddenly realized he had never kissed her and now he obviously wanted to very badly. The part of her mind that wasn't occupied with devising a slow, painful death for Race Bennett considered the situation. It came to her that she must be slightly drunk or she would have been thinking more clearly. Dean had been romantic, tender and attentive all evening; he had taken her out for a candlelight dinner and bought her flowers. Of course that had all been leading up to something.

"Vicky, I wasn't just trying to turn your head when I said you were beautiful. You're the most beautiful woman I've ever seen. I mean that."

"You do?" she asked weakly.

He reached out to touch her soft cheek. A warm smile curved his mouth. "Yes, I do. Even when you're hot and dirty and wearing old kennel clothes."

"Oh."

This date had been a dreadful mistake. How could she have agreed to such a stupid idea? Dean leaned toward her with passionate intent, and Vicky wondered what she was doing sitting with this man in a dark car in a storm. How on earth was she going to get away without hurting his feelings or insulting his manhood? Had Dean always been this boring? She thought she used to like him at least a little more than this. But that had been before Race and his dark fire, before his hot kisses and unlikely halo, before the demanding delight of his hands on her body, seeking and knowing....

"Where are you?" whispered Dean.

"I'm right here," she answered, puzzled.

He pulled away slightly to look into her face.

"No," he said. "You're a thousand miles away. It's hard not to notice when the woman in your company isn't thinking of you."

Vicky's cheeks burned with shame. "I'm sorry, Dean," she whispered. There was a long pause.

"Is it me?" he asked gently.

"No."

"Is it Race, then?"

"Race? What does he have to do with this?" she asked defensively.

"Something about the way he looks at you—"

"I have nothing to do with him. He's my—my silent partner, and that's all," she insisted emphatically.

"Then what is it, Vicky? Is it something I can change?"

She touched his face gently, wondering what on earth she could tell him. "I like you very much. You know that, Dean. I guess there's just no chemistry between us. Anyhow, with Hank gone, I have so much on my mind, I have no strength for a personal life."

He let out a long sigh and rested his forehead against hers. "If that's the way you really feel, then I suppose I can't change it. But I think you have enough strength for anything, Vicky, and I'll keep hoping that someday you'll feel the . . . chemistry that I do."

She was about to respond when the car door flew open. Rain splashed her startled face as she turned out of Dean's embrace. It was too dark to see more than Race's outline, but she knew who it was before he spoke.

"Sorry to interrupt," he said in a voice of deadly calm as the rain drenched him, "but the storm's expected to get worse before it gets better. You'd best be on your way if you don't want to get wrapped around a tree, Doc. Come on, Vicky." Something about his tone, his stance and the subtle threat in his statement encouraged immediate cooperation from her. She was, in any event, glad to make a swift exit from the delicate scene.

"Good night, Dean. Thanks for—for everything."

"Don't mention it," said Dean ruefully. "You'll take care of her, Race?"

"Oh, yes. I certainly will," said Race laconically. He pulled Vicky out of the car and slammed the door.

They stood in the rain and watched the car go. Vicky was immensely relieved that the evening was over, and very sorry she hadn't handled it better. Dean was a good man, and she had probably made him feel like a panting teenager making heavy passes. And she was sure it was somehow all Race's fault. She was soaking wet, and that was his fault, too, she decided unreasonably, since he had dragged her out of the car and into the pouring rain.

"What the hell are you wearing?" Race asked rudely.

"It's a dress. I do own a few, you know. And Dean thinks I look beautiful in this one," she snapped at him. She looked down at her long body. The rain had plastered the pale silk against her torso and thighs, showing every line and curve in bold detail. She glanced back up to find Race looking down at her glistening body as well. She couldn't see his expression, but a sudden, forbidden heat flowed through her.

"I'm going home," she announced.

"No, you're not," he said brusquely, and grabbed her arm. "If you don't get knocked on the head by a falling branch or blown off the bridge by the wind or hit by lightning—" an angry flash appeared in the sky, followed by a loud explosion "—you'll certainly drown in the mud." He started dragging her toward the house.

"But Rebel—"

"I fed her and put her inside the kennel an hour ago!"

"I'm not coming with you!"

"Oh, yes, you are," he said grimly, and hauled her to the front door. Vicky twisted and squirmed, yanked his arm and dragged her feet. She was astonished to find it had no effect on him. She was stronger than many men and wasn't accustomed to being manhandled by someone much stronger than she.

Race pulled her inside and slammed the door shut against the wind. He finally let go of Vicky, and they regarded each other with hostility as water dripped from their bodies. She turned away and went to the vast window in the living room to look out at the night. The sky was lit again and again with angry streaks of light, each followed by a violent explosion. The wind blew the oak trees fiercely. A tree branch crashed to the ground and a canvas chair went rolling across the lawn. Rain beat noisily against the roof and windows. All of nature was in turmoil out there, as if the gods were venting their rage on the transgressing humans who now sought shelter wherever they could find it.

She turned to see Race lighting candles and placing them around the room.

"The electric lines went?" she asked loudly, trying to be heard above the storm.

He nodded curtly. His every gesture contained a caged, barely suppressed fury. "About twenty minutes ago. Just before you got home. What were you thinking of, necking out there in the middle of this storm like a witless teenager?"

His words stung her into renewed fury. "What gives you the right to talk to me that way? Or to yank me out of the car and drag me inside as if I were a kid breaking curfew?"

"If you want privacy next time, why don't you park somewhere other than right in front of my living-room window? Or do you enjoy an audience?" he shot back.

"You bastard!" Vicky's jaw dropped a split second later as she realized what she'd called him.

"I've never denied it," he agreed with grim irony. "And who really knows how many others he sired? Did you ever think you might bear one of them yourself, Vicky?"

"What are you talking about?" she spat out.

"You and my father. What did you give him to make him give you all this?"

Vicky's eyes flew open with rage and shock and insult. "Nothing! Nothing! I never—I never—"

"And what about our friendly neighborhood vet?" he continued in growing fury.

"Stop it!" she shouted.

"I'm just getting started! How does it work, Vicky? Did you keep Hank twisted up in knots, like me and your clean-cut vet? Did you hold out on him all those years, letting him watch you and want you, letting him believe he could have you if he just gave you everything you wanted?"

"No! You don't—"

"Do I have to give you everything before you'll—"

"I hate you!" Vicky shouted furiously. She hit Race as hard as she could, so hard his head turned sideways with the force of the blow. She stared at him in shocked, unthinking silence for a moment before panic overtook her and she tried to run from him.

Race seized her in his strong arms, trying to subdue her without hurting her as she struggled wildly. A blind rage like none she'd ever known burned through her, making her want to hit and kick and scream, making her want to wound and hurt him the way he'd hurt her.

Race shouted, trying to be heard above the raging storm and Vicky's own infuriated, incoherent cries, but she didn't know or care what he was saying. Finally he got the upper hand and she was effectively stilled, her energy spent, her arms pinned to her sides in his tight embrace.

Vicky panted with exhaustion and hysteria. She gulped in air, her breasts heaving against his chest. The face she turned up to his was harrowed and streaked with tears of rage and hurt.

"It wasn't like that; it wasn't! *I'm* not like that," she insisted tearfully, willing him to believe her and agree.

"What was it like?" His voice was almost as breathless as hers.

"You don't want to know! Let go of me!" She struggled again.

One strong hand twisted into her tumbled hair and pulled her head back, forcing her to meet his angry gray eyes.

"What are *you* like?" he demanded in a low voice burning with the frustration of long-suppressed passion. "You look at me with blazing green eyes; you touch me like a hungry witch; you laugh with me like a child—and every time I come close to you, you shove me away and say no, because I won't let you have everything your own way regardless of the consequences. What do you think you're playing at? Do you think I'm one of your pets, that you can call all the shots and then throw me a treat in exchange for unquestioning obedience?"

"No!" she said hotly.

His hand moved from her hair to roughly stroke her face and neck. She shuddered and closed her eyes, instinctively and unwillingly giving herself up to the harsh caresses of that strong, callused hand.

"How many men have you tamed that way, Vicky? How many have given in to those green, green eyes?"

She saw the naked desire in his eyes, felt the urgency in his long, taut body, sensed the pent-up longing in his touch. It echoed her own unruly, ungovernable desires. A strangled moan escaped her before she strained upward to press her mouth against his warm, firm lips. He answered her touch at once, sliding his tongue into her mouth without hesitation. Then a rigid stillness seized him. He pulled away from her roughly.

"You're drunk," he said tightly. "I don't want—"

But Vicky slid her arms out of his restraining hold and reached up to insistently pull his head down to hers before he had time to order her away. As her tongue brushed his lips, Race shuddered, then wrapped her in an embrace tight enough to suffocate a more fragile woman.

The howling storm outside suddenly paled in comparison to the storm raging between Vicky and Race. There was no peace between them, no gentleness or tenderness. They touched and kissed each other with a wild hunger, with a ruthless demand born of fear and longing and jealousy.

Under the cover of wind and thunder, she could hear Race muttering fierce, feverish words she didn't understand fully;

they frightened her and thrilled her, making her want to run from him, making her want to become part of him.

In the shadowy room they tore wildly at each other's clothes with no thought to ever putting them on again. The lightning illuminated their bodies for each other in tantalizing, confusing flashes as material ripped and buttons went flying.

Then Race was carrying her across the room, lifting her as easily as if she were a child, to lie with her on the thick Persian rug.

They made love to each other with total abandon, with a wild passion free of shyness or rules. Vicky moaned and writhed luxuriously as Race's hot lips teased the taut peaks of her breasts, stroked her smooth belly, kissed the soft skin of her thighs and the ultrasensitive flesh between them; and she knew that in every hot kiss, in every teasing flick of his satiny tongue, he sought to torment her as much as to pleasure her.

They rolled over and over on the soft rug, delighting in their absolute freedom to touch and admire each other, to give and to take pleasure. Vicky covered Race's hard chest with fevered kisses, hungrily tasting his salty skin, touching him as if she were starved for him. She slid her hand down to the dark hair between his legs and possessively wrapped her fingers around him, unconsciously rough in her passion. Race shuddered, his groan one of mingled pain and pleasure. His fingers dug into Vicky's soft, pale skin. He slipped his hand down to close over hers and kissed her demandingly, his lips hard and seeking, his tongue urging hers insistently.

Race pushed Vicky onto her back and rolled over on top of her. Their joined hands guided his flesh to hers, to where her body was made for this, only for this. She raised her hips to meet his deep, strong thrusts, wrapping her arms and legs around him as if he were a demon lover who might try to escape before pleasuring her. He let her take the full weight of his body, pressing her into the floor, and she held him tighter, as if she could draw his soul into her body.

There was no thought or knowledge or self-control. Vicky would have forgotten her own name if he weren't moaning it harshly, warmly, achingly, again and again. She had never known anything like this. No one had ever touched her like this, had ever invited and demanded her most hidden, savage passions this way. No one had ever frightened her, thrilled her, moved her like this. She caressed the flexing muscles of his back and shoulders, returned the sweet kisses of his seeking lips, heaved wildly in their erotic mating dance. The rhythm of their passion and tortured sighs was echoed in the drumming rain, and the thunder answered Race's harsh, ragged breath.

They soared together to a stormy heaven as lightning streaked the angry sky, illuminating their arched, gleaming bodies and the fiercely passionate expressions on their faces.

It seemed a long time later that Vicky finally tumbled back to earth. Race was still on top of her, his heavy body crushing hers in a pleasing way. His hand was stroking her hair gently, and he was kissing her neck with a tenderness they had eschewed only moments before. She turned her head slightly and nuzzled his hair. She stroked his back lightly, caressing the hot skin over his smooth muscles. They stayed like that for long minutes without speaking, only caressing each other tenderly, reassuring each other with touch, as if to make up for the violence with which they had used each other.

Finally he lifted his head and his eyes met hers. He and Vicky regarded each other seriously, almost curiously, stunned by what they had just done together. Surely, she thought, there could be few secrets left between people who had taken each other with such primitive savagery.

"I've never done anything like this before," she whispered.

"Neither have I," answered Race softly.

She touched him gently, feeling that after what she'd just done to him, she must own his body in a way. She hadn't known she was capable of anything like that, hadn't realized just how deep and wild her passions could run. She was almost frightened of what she had discovered tonight. But the pleasure was too strong to allow fear much importance.

As if he had followed her thoughts, Race kissed her gently and said, "I'm glad you're an Amazon woman. I'd have probably broken a few of your ribs if you'd been a little weak thing. I'm sorry I was so rough."

"I was rough, too. I guess we're not quite ourselves tonight."

"Or maybe we're more ourselves than we've ever been," Race answered.

Vicky shifted uncomfortably under his penetrating perusal. She was remembering how this had all started.

"There was never anything... like that between me and Hank," she said, her eyes meeting his candidly. "He was like a father to me. He was more of a father to me than my real father. There was never even once a hint of anything else between us. We acted like—like you and Wade together. I loved him, Race. I gave him all the love I could never give my own parents, all the love he thought he never got from his real kids. I know he had a lot of faults—he did wrong by your mother—but sometimes I just miss him so much...."

To her chagrin, she started crying. Race rolled over on his back and held her against his chest, wrapped in his arms. He squeezed her comfortingly and kissed her hair, holding her like that until her tears subsided. And if he knew that she cried for herself and him as well as for Hank, he asked no questions.

It was much later, as the storm was letting up, that Race apologized for his angry words.

"I knew Hank had a way with women," he said. He was apparently oblivious to the fact that he had inherited it, she thought wryly. "My mom was a smart woman, but she loved him for years anyhow, and she always said Eleanore did, too. And I wasn't exaggerating when I said I might not be his only bastard. There was always someone in his life. You must have known that."

"I noticed it after a while."

"So when I got here and saw you, I just figured ... His taste in women was always good, you know."

"But, Race, he was old enough to be my father! He was *older* than my father!"

"That's never stopped people before, Vicky."

"And you honestly thought I was his mistress?"

"I thought so at first. But the better I got to know you, the less I believed it. I guess I've known for a long time that you weren't his woman. I just didn't know what you were instead. I lost my head tonight." He added wryly, "I used to be such a reasonable person until I met you."

"That's not the way Wade makes it sound," she reminded him.

Race smiled but didn't answer. Mentioning Wade made Vicky think of Race's life in California. She could have bitten her tongue off as soon as she asked her next question.

"Who's Karen?"

He had been studying her naked body with interest. Now he looked up with a puzzled frown. "Karen? She's my secretary. Why?"

Vicky felt a rush of relief. "No reason. What did she want?"

"Jealous, Vicky? This is coals of fire indeed. She just wanted to know how things are going out here. I told her she should probably start looking for a new job, since I hope I may have reason to stay here for good."

Vicky felt as if he'd slapped her. He was that certain she'd lose everything. She hoped by now he knew her well enough to know she wouldn't give up without a fight. He'd stripped her raw tonight and opened up new and old wounds. Despite the physical satiation of her desires, there was an aching void inside herself she didn't understand. And the unbearable pressure of it made the possibility of losing Oak Hill seem like the end of the world tonight.

She sat up uncomfortably, feeling nervous and exposed. Race was studying her with those searching, smoky eyes.

"Vicky—"

"I have to go see if everything's all right at the kennel."
She stood up and reached for her dress. He followed her and
watched with brooding eyes while she tried to arrange its
torn fragments on her body.

"It's the middle of the night," he pointed out.

"I don't want to wait till morning," she lied. "It's probably total chaos over there."

"I'll come with you," he said, reaching for his trousers.

"No, don't." He waited for her to explain. "I—I think I
need to be alone for a while. This...what happened tonight hasn't really changed anything, Race."

His eyes narrowed dangerously. "Hasn't it?"

"Can I borrow this? My dress won't...won't..." She
slipped his ripped shirt around her shoulders and left the
house in a hurry, aware of his penetrating stare following her
out the door.

She ran down the familiar path, seeking anonymity in the
dark woods, seeking a place to hide from him and from
herself. Because she knew as well as he did that tonight had
changed everything.

Seven

Nadine usually came to work well before dawn to bathe and groom any boarders checking out that morning. She found Vicky wandering around the kennel in the early hours, doing innumerable heavy chores that really could have waited till daylight. Vicky saw Nadine's eyes take in her torn clothing, covered by Race's ripped shirt, her mussed hair, swollen lips and haunted eyes.

"Race?" said Nadine matter-of-factly.

Vicky nodded wearily.

"It's about time. You two have been circling each other since he got here. Vicky, don't treat it like such a *tragedy*."

"He wants my kennel."

Nadine shook her head in exasperation. "There's something else he wants, too, you *idiot*. But you're too over-worked and overwrought to see it."

"My money," Vicky said glumly.

"Vicky, you're a good kennel manager and you've got the best touch with dogs of anyone I've ever seen, but you're a damned *fool* when it comes to men."

Vicky started to cry. Nadine held her in a sisterly hug and told her to let it all out. She finally gave Vicky a grooming towel to dry her eyes on. She examined with curiosity Vicky's torn clothes and exhausted expression.

"You should see the other guy," Vicky joked feebly.

"You two really took it out on each other, didn't you?"

Vicky took a piping-hot shower in the grooming room and then went home to change before the rest of her staff arrived at 7:00 a.m. Every inch of her body ached, and she could only hope Race felt as sore as she did. She had worked herself to exhaustion during the night; she always thought most clearly when engaged in heavy physical labor. But tonight it had not helped. She was still confused and scared.

Every time she closed her eyes she saw Race's dark head, hair shining like burnished gold in the candlelight, bent over her body with punishing, enrapturing intent. He had woven a spell around her she feared she could never break. He had touched the darkest corners of her soul in the stormy night, had turned the world upside down and left her shaken and disoriented. She only knew that making love with him was like drinking from the sea; sating her desires had only made her hunger for him more.

Vicky and her staff finished clearing up the fallen branches and scattered debris left by the storm and returned to a normal working day. She was dressed more modestly than usually but still couldn't hide all the marks of Race's passion on her body. The look on her face, however, completely discouraged any curious or teasing comments.

It was Ginny who brought the bad news. She came into the kennel with a handful of newspapers and a grim expression, muttering angrily about busybodies and scandalmongers.

Vicky's name appeared in, of all places, the society column. The article explained that the Washington community was "astir" to discover that the late and eminently respected Henry Race had left his property in Virginia to the beautiful redheaded Victoria Wood, nearly forty years his

junior. And what had this voluptuous young woman done
for Henry Race, to have merited such generous consider-
ation? Even more astonishing was the fact that Miss Wood
now jointly owned the property with *Race* Bennett, who,
according to the rumors, was more closely related to Henry
Race than was Miss Wood, though not more legally. The
two young people were evidently cohabiting in lush, se-
cluded Oak Hill now. Like father, like son ... One couldn't
help wondering what Henry Race's widow, Eleanore,
thought about all this....

Vicky exploded with rage and threw the paper across the
room. She threw a few food bowls against the wall, and they
made a satisfying clatter. She picked up a fifty-pound bag
of dog food and threw it as hard as she could. It landed with
a resounding thud and split wide open, scattering dry meal
all over the floor. She surveyed the wreckage with dismay.
Then she looked at Ginny's stack of newspapers.

"They all say the same thing?"

"Almost word for word. Some of them mention Hank's
wicked ways as well."

Vicky groaned. "This is all I need right now." She sat
down and put her head in her hands. "Do you know it never
occurred to me that anyone would ever think such a thing?
It's so obvious! Why did it never occur to me?"

"Because it would never occur to any decent person,"
said Ginny in a soothing, motherly tone as she put an arm
around Vicky.

"Oh, come on, Ginny! I'll bet it's occurred to everyone
who knows me," Vicky said tiredly. It had occurred to Race,
she thought.

"Not to us. Hank treated you like a favorite daughter. We
all knew that. Some folks just can't understand that something honest and real could take hold of someone as jaded
as Hank."

"Thank you, Ginny," Vicky mumbled, grateful for the
support of the people nearest her.

Word spread quickly after that. Journalists, reporters and
columnists kept telephoning Vicky to ask her to make a

statement or consent to an interview. She kept saying no. She didn't want to do anything until she talked to Race, and he had disappeared; the house was empty and his car was gone.

The six o'clock news at the kennel was a shock to Vicky. The story was getting TV coverage! Brief but humiliating. There was a quick explanation of the situation, a few shots of Vicky in her usual skimpy outfit that had been taken around the Fourth of July, and then a clip of a bunch of journalists accosting Eleanore outside her Georgetown home.

Eleanore looked as elegant as ever, Vicky saw. Although Eleanore was in her late fifties, her figure and face had maintained their firmness. Her hair was ice blond, and as she answered impertinent questions, her eyes were ice blue. She would issue no statement until she had spoken with her lawyers.

Vicky was scared. Now they had offended Eleanore and her family. There would be hell to pay. Vicky would rather have faced a whole kennelful of snarling, hysterical dogs than tangle with Hank's family. Where was Race when she needed him, dammit? He still hadn't returned. More than anything in the world, she wanted to feel his strong arms wrapped around her and the steady, reassuring stroke of his hands on her hair.

Tears of worry and frustration spilled from her eyes to trace a path down her cheeks. She heard a footstep behind her. Race! She turned eagerly to greet him, then felt her face fall in disappointment.

"Vicky!" Dean exclaimed. "I would have come sooner, but I couldn't get away. It's all over town. Are you all right?" The gentle concern in his face shamed her, especially since she had bluntly rejected his affections only last night. Last night? It seemed an aeon ago.

"I'm all right, Dean," she said, wiping her tears away. "It's just . . . I just . . ." She lowered her head miserably.

Dean touched her arm lightly. "Need a shoulder to cry on? Just one friend to another?"

Vicky gratefully came into his arms, accepting his warm comfort. It was relaxing, but his touch couldn't chase away the clouds of disaster looming over her head. She burrowed closer to him, unsuccessfully trying to shed the icy dread that gripped her. She spoke softly, droning on about what Eleanore would do to her, about how much she wished Hank were still here, about how it would kill her to lose the kennel.

Suddenly Dean's whole body tensed. "Hello, Race," he said calmly but without warmth.

Vicky raised her head to see Race standing a few feet away from them. His whole body was rigid; his eyes were narrowed; his face was dark and closed. He seemed almost carved out of stone. There was no trace of the man she knew.

"I was worried about Vicky," Race said. His voice was flat, completely without emotion. "I can see she's in good hands, so I'll be on my way." He left abruptly.

Dean released Vicky as she pulled away and distractedly thanked him for his support.

"I hope I haven't caused trouble between you and Race," he said quietly.

Vicky smiled without humor. "The sun rising in the east could cause trouble between me and Race."

She saw Dean to the front door, assuring him she would be perfectly all right on her own. And in fact it was true; she left Brian and Désirée to lock up and stumbled home to her cottage, too numb to feel anything but the desire to sleep. She fed Rebel, showered again and tumbled into bed, falling into virtual unconsciousness.

In the ebony, still hours that precede the dawn, when the body is most greedy for sleep, a strong hand shook Vicky's shoulder. She struck out sleepily with a hard fist.

"Vicky!" Race's exasperated voice brought her to consciousness. He was sitting on her bed in the dark, his hair rumpled with sleep, his hastily donned shirt hanging open.

"Race? What are you doing here?" she asked sleepily. "How'd you get in?"

"Your door was open. Do you always sleep so heavily?"

"No, of course not. In case you've forgotten, I didn't sleep at all last night," she said irritably.

"I haven't forgotten." His eyes lowered to where the sheet had fallen away, and he noted her soft white skin and the faint marks left on it by their passion. Vicky's own gaze strayed over him, studying the body she'd learned so thoroughly the night before. There was a strange kind of peace between them when their eyes met again.

"I think there's trouble at the kennel. The lights are on; everybody's barking."

"Oh, no!" She leaped out of bed and threw on clothes as Race handed them to her. His eyes widened slightly at the dainty, lacy panties he passed to her—a birthday gift from Nadine—but he didn't say anything.

The last thing she needed, the last thing she could handle, was trouble at the kennel now. With the airline strike and Race Bennett, the media and Eleanore Race all breathing down her neck, she really couldn't take any more.

Vicky barely paused to pull on her sneakers, then she and Race were tearing down the path, his hand holding hers to keep her from falling down in the dark. As they approached the kennel, they could see that the lights were on in the back hallway and the lounge. The dogs were barking uproariously, thrilled to see a change in their routine. Rebel assumed it was all a new nocturnal game and kept trying to knock Vicky down, which did not improve Vicky's disposition.

The most notable cause of disturbance was a very large man pounding furiously on the front door and demanding to be let in. His face was obscured by shadows, but the moonlight glinted menacingly off a long, smooth object cradled in his right arm.

Vicky's jaw dropped in astonishment. She pulled Race to a halt by the side door and whispered, "That's a... Isn't that a...?"

"Shotgun," Race agreed. "Come on—get inside."

They slipped into the building through the side door—which should have been locked, Vicky realized worriedly. They raced toward the lounge, which seemed to be the center of all the confusion. When they got there, Vicky stopped so abruptly she would have fallen over if Race hadn't still been holding her hand.

Brian was standing on top of two precariously balanced chairs and trying to pry open a skylight that had been painted shut the year before, while Désirée ran around the room, wringing her hands, crying hysterically and gibbering about his imminent death.

"Brian!" Vicky gaped at him.

Désirée shrieked, and Brian and his stacked chairs came toppling to the floor with a heavy thud that made Race wince.

Brian jumped to his feet almost as quickly as he'd fallen. "Vicky! Don't scare me like that, man!"

"Brian, what are you doing? What's going on here?" Vicky demanded.

Brian's face screwed up and his mouth worked silently; Vicky wasn't sure if he was praying or trying to come up with an explanation he thought she would believe. Désirée continued to cry and wring her hands, giving a good impression of what Vicky considered the ultimate in useless, pretty heroines.

Finally Brian threw his hands up in defeat and looked pleadingly at Race. Vicky glanced from Brian's haggard expression to Désirée's luscious body and puffy face, and realization dawned.

"Oh, Brian, how could you? Don't you know we can't afford any more scandal right now?" Vicky cried despairingly.

"Honestly, Vicky, nothing happened. We were just... um..." Brian's tongue failed him again.

"Exploring the richness and depths of each other's minds, I'm sure," Vicky finished sarcastically.

"Something like that," Brian mumbled.

"Did you even bother to get any work done?" Vicky demanded.

"Well—"

"Never mind that now," interrupted Race. The pounding on the front door had grown louder, and the man outside was fairly roaring with rage. "I take it that man is Désirée's father."

Désirée let out a howl of anguish, and Brian nodded resignedly. "We were trying to find a way to get out of here without being seen. I thought maybe if he didn't actually find us here together he'd think he'd just made a mistake...."

Vicky's deadpan expression told Brian what she thought of the cleverness of *that* plan. "Perhaps you should have simply made sure Désirée got home before three o'clock in the morning, Brian."

"Is that what time it is? Gosh, Mom will be worried! If you'll excuse me, Vicky, I think I'll just—"

"I think you're too late," Race warned as Brian tried to climb back up to the skylight. Désirée's father started throwing himself against the door, and it seemed clear that the lock was never meant to take that much abuse and wouldn't hold out much longer.

"What are we going to do?" Vicky asked frantically.

"Call the cops," urged Brian while Désirée sobbed more loudly.

"And have this appear in all the papers tomorrow? I'd rather see you shot full of lead first," Vicky answered.

"He's got a shotgun," Race reminded her. Brian turned an unbecoming shade of green. Vicky realized how serious the situation was becoming. Race switched off the lights.

"What are you doing?" she asked.

"Evening the odds. He can't see his target so well in the dark."

"Maybe I *should* call the police," she conceded.

The question became academic at that point, as the door burst open and Désirée's father stampeded through the lobby. Désirée fainted.

"Get her out of here," Race ordered Brian softly. "We'll handle this."

"We will?" Vicky whispered nervously.

Brian tried to drag Désirée's prone form out of the room. The moonlight caught his blond hair, and the outraged father saw it as soon as he turned the corner.

"There you are, you young devil! Drop her!"

"Drop?" Brian croaked.

"I told you what I'd do if I caught you with my daughter again!"

He raised the shotgun purposefully. He hadn't seen Vicky or Race in the dark, and they used surprise to their advantage. Vicky threw herself at him bodily, screaming for Brian to run. Race grabbed the shotgun as the man tumbled to the ground with Vicky on top of him. The two of them wrestled earnestly for a moment while Brian abandoned Désirée to her fate and obeyed Vicky's orders to run. Race turned the light on and pointed the shotgun straight at Désirée's father.

"You hurt one hair on her pretty little head and I'll fill you full of holes," Race warned in a fair imitation of the man's accent.

"Miss Wood!" said Désirée's father in astonishment. He released his strategic grip on her body. "Beg your pardon, ma'am," he said in embarrassment.

"No harm done," said Vicky as she got to her feet. She caught Race's eye and whispered accusingly, "You're enjoying this."

"What teamwork," he said. But his face took on a puzzled look as he examined the shotgun. "It's not loaded."

"Course not! I could hurt someone!" Désirée's father was shocked at the implication.

"Why do you carry around a shotgun if you don't mean to shoot anybody?" demanded Race.

"To make these young fellers see I mean business." He spotted Désirée's prone body, voluptuous even in her unconsciousness, and gave a martyred sigh. "Can you imagine what it's like to have such a daughter?"

"Doesn't the girl's mother have any influence over her?" Race asked.

"Ran off with a hairdresser ten years ago. Good riddance. That woman cost me more worry than a keg of dynamite. I'll just be glad when this one gets married off and I can go back to normal living for the first time in twenty years."

"Well, she may quiet down after this. I think all the commotion tonight upset her quite a bit," Race assured him. "I don't think there's any need to punish—"

"Punish her? I've never laid a hand to that child in my life! It's that young devil who was with her that could use a good licking!" insisted the father.

"I think Miss Wood will see that he gets what's coming to him, sir. Never fear," Race said dryly. Vicky nodded emphatically.

She felt rather sorry for the poor man. Going around beating up the local boys wasn't the way to deal with the situation, but he was a simple man trying to protect Désirée's health and reputation as he saw fit. Vicky assured him that there was no reason for Désirée to stop working at Oak Hill. Despite certain problems, the girl was a hard worker with a lot of stamina and a genuine liking for dogs. And Vicky felt quite sure that Brian would not repeat his mistake. Race listened sympathetically to the man's troubles while she ruthlessly slapped Désirée awake and helped her out to her father's car. Vicky wished the turbulent family a good-night and reminded Désirée she was expected back at work the following day to wash down all four wings with flea-and-tick dip.

Race was examining the broken lock when Vicky came back inside. He promised to fix it first thing in the morning, assuring her it would be inexpensive to replace.

In the quiet of the empty lobby her eyes met his gray ones for a still moment before she and Race both burst out laughing.

"What a night!" she exclaimed. "I'm glad you were here, Race. I'm not sure what I would have done, faced on my own with teenage love and an angry, gun-toting father."

"I think you'd have done just fine. What a tackle!" he said, reminding her of her unthinking leap at Désirée's father in the dark. "But I'm glad I was here to lend a hand."

Something warm, like true friendship, flowed easily between them. The moment was too sweet to let go, so Vicky offered to make him a cup of coffee in the kitchen. Nadine entered the building a few minutes later. She joined Race and Vicky for coffee while they gave her a brief account of the night's events.

"Doesn't anyone around here ever *sleep* anymore?" Nadine asked disgustedly, and went off to her grooming room to start work.

"Where were you all day?" Vicky asked Race as soon as they were alone.

"With lawyers." His tone indicated that he hadn't enjoyed it much. "As soon as I saw the papers I went into the city to talk it over with them to find out if there's anything we can do."

"I want to sue them for every penny they've got!"

"Hank's lawyer advised us to keep quiet. I don't think he likes you, Vicky. What did you do to him? No, don't answer that. I can guess. So then I went to see my old college friend, who, as it happens, is a lawyer. She advises you to issue a clear statement about your relationship with Hank. She says as long as he never spent the night with you, there can be no—"

"But he did."

"What?"

"I mean, he used to spend the night at my house. Often. Whenever he was here and it was too late to drive back to the city, he would sleep on my couch. Everyone knew...." Vicky's eyes widened in dismay as she realized the implication.

"Oh, Vicky." Race tiredly rubbed a hand across his forehead.

"Race, *you* believe—"

"Of course I believe you. Let's just hope we can convince everyone else."

"We?"

"You didn't think I'd throw you to the wolves, did you?"

Their eyes met in warm communication. She suddenly felt a little braver.

"I'm glad you're here," she said softly.

It seemed the most natural thing in the world to lean forward and kiss him. Race hesitated for a moment, then drew her into his arms. Their bodies fit together perfectly, their hands knew just how to please each other, their sweet kisses started a warm glow inside Vicky's weary body. His arms tightened around her, and the worries of the day retreated and dimmed as she had known they would. She ran her fingers through his shiny hair and pressed her mouth more firmly against his.

"For shame, you two! Don't you know we can't afford any more scandal right now?"

Vicky whirled out of Race's arms to see Brian grinning broadly at them. She felt herself blush like a schoolgirl and tried to pull together her bosslike dignity.

"Where have you been hiding?" asked Race.

"In Myron's run. Safest place in the whole kennel," answered Brian. "A man would have to be crazy to follow me in there."

Remembering the enthusiastic Saint Bernard who had flattened him his first day at Oak Hill, Race could not but agree. Brian looked distinctly disheveled and had big paw prints all over his body.

"You have got a lot of explaining to do, young man," Vicky warned Brian.

"I know, I know. Vicky, I really am sorry about this. It would never have happened if she weren't so...if she didn't have..."

"I think we get the picture," Race said dryly.

"But there's to be no more of this sort of thing around here," Vicky insisted.

"Are you kidding? Wild horses couldn't get me near that girl again," Brian promised. Then a wistful look came into his eyes. "But she sure has the most incredible—"

"Yes. Well, why don't you go along home now and try to explain this to your mother. I'll talk to you in the morning. And I'll have a nice long list of chores to keep your mind occupied for the next few weeks."

"Yes, Vicky." Brian sighed. "Thanks for not firing me, anyhow." A wicked glint came into his eyes as he advised Race, "She's pretty attached to me, you know."

"Out!" Vicky ordered.

After Brian left, Race broke the worst news of the night to Vicky.

"Hank's lawyer advises us to get a lawyer of our own."

"Why?"

"Eleanore's thinking of contesting the will, and she's been his client for twenty years."

"Oh, no," Vicky groaned. "I knew it. I knew it. What are we going to do? Can she take Oak Hill away from us?"

"My friend says she'll be happy to represent us. But she'll need all the facts before she can advise us or give an opinion."

Vicky nodded. She sat lost in thought for a while. When she looked up, she saw Race brooding as well.

"And you?" she asked. "If they offer us money to give up Oak Hill and disappear, will you take it and go home? Or do you want to fight to keep it?"

"I'm staying," he said firmly. His eyes were calm and determined. Then one side of his mouth lifted in that private smile he sometimes had. "I'm a damned fool, but I can't help it. We'll see this thing through together, Vicky."

She smiled warmly and gratefully at him, forgetting for a moment that he, too, wanted to take the kennel away from her. But they were at least united in their love of this land and their determination to keep it. Race might have come here as a stranger with vague boyhood memories, but Oak Hill's lush green beauty in the sultry summer was seducing him, too, and she knew he thought of it as home now.

Nadine came back into the kitchen. "Vicky, you look like *death*, my dear. Race, just look at those circles under her eyes. I ask you, is that an appealing sight? Vicky, do go to bed before you keel over! Who's going to hold things together if you make yourself sick?"

Vicky rolled her eyes. Race smiled wryly at her.

"Nadine's right," he said. "You go home and go back to bed. I'll lock up."

Eight

There was at least some good news to greet Vicky at the kennel the next morning: the airline strike was over. It had lasted only three days! The phone was ringing off the hook with customers eager to cancel their cancellations, as it were, and take off as soon as possible.

Ironically the scandal surrounding Vicky's relationship with Henry Race and her joint inheritance with Race Bennett turned out to be a boon for the kennel. Granted, a few people did cancel reservations and appointments with venomous remarks about Vicky's morals and reputation, but by and large people were far more curious than shocked. People who had never heard of Oak Hill Pet Motel and normally left their dogs with other kennels or with their relatives now flocked to Vicky's place. Some people had barely absorbed the sensational story but had simply seen a boarding kennel plastered all over the newspapers and TV screen just when they happened to need one. Many others, however, obviously wanted to combine business with pleasure and came with the hope of seeing something that was worth repeating to their friends. Vicky's presence had never before been requested so often in the lobby. "May I speak with the owner?" was the catchphrase of the week. Everyone found some cause, however trivial, to speak with Vicky, and she noticed their eyes roam avidly over every inch of her as they asked idle questions or made unfounded complaints.

Vicky herself would have been almost glad it had all happened if the scandal wasn't likely to produce such disastrous consequences between her and Eleanore. She didn't care what people thought of her; she assumed most humans were insincere and selfish to begin with and so she had no illusions that could be shattered by avid stares and insolent questions. Because of her height and unusual appearance, she was even used to being stared at, though perhaps not as frequently as this.

In fact, the only thing that shook her cool was the unexpected warmth and support of her staff, local people and even some of her customers. Two days after the story first appeared in the papers, Mr. Lyons, the customer she had lectured at length before unloading the food truck, nearly reduced her to sentimental tears.

Vicky was in the far left wing with Désirée. Seen from a distance, Désirée looked quite normal, but as soon as anyone approached her she turned scarlet with embarrassment and seemed incapable of speech. The story of her misadventures had, of course, spread. Vicky had been too preoccupied to gossip, but Nadine had told the story to the rest of the staff in lavish detail. If Désirée's father was to be believed, this sort of thing probably happened to her a lot, and she would bounce back to normal in a day or two. Brian, on the other hand, turned white as a sheet every time someone mentioned fathers, guns or police. Vicky was profoundly glad she was no longer seventeen.

"What do you mean, 'the water's funny'?" Vicky was demanding impatiently now.

Désirée mumbled something to the ground.

"For Pete's sake, speak up!" Vicky insisted above the roar of fifty happy dogs.

"I mean it's funny. Sometimes it's all right; sometimes it won't come and sometimes it's too strong. It's funny."

Oak Hill was totally reliant on its water supply and any serious problems could cripple the whole operation. "All right. I'll call the plumber and tell him to come out today. Is this happening in all the wings?"

"No. Just this one."

Ginny's voice boomed over the intercom, asking Vicky to come to the lobby.

"Oh, brother, another gaper," muttered Vicky irritably, and made her way to the front of the kennel.

When she arrived, Race was already in the lobby, trying to break up a sudden disagreement between an Irish setter and a schnauzer. Vicky grabbed the schnauzer from behind, deftly avoiding its hysterically snappy jaws, and the fight came to an undignified end. Race comforted the trembling, cowed Irish setter and handed it back to its owner.

"I suggest you bring a leash with you if you can't control a little dog like this," Vicky said rudely as she handed the schnauzer back to its elegant owner. The woman was clearly too interested in examining Vicky to respond.

"Why is it the little ones are the meanest?" Race asked Vicky with a grin.

"I guess they have to be tougher to protect themselves," she answered. "Who wanted to see me?"

"I did," said Mr. Lyons. "How are you today, Vicky?"

"I'm fine, Mr. Lyons. And you?"

"Just terrific. And you, Race?"

Having proved he was on first-name terms with the owners, Mr. Lyons now had the attention of an entire lobbyful of customers, Vicky observed.

"Just fine, sir. What kind of dog is that?" said Race.

"It's a saluki," said Vicky automatically. "Probably the oldest known breed. They were used as hunting dogs by the ancient Egyptians."

"That's our Vicky," Mr. Lyons said, chuckling. His conversational tone included the other customers now.

"This young lady knows enough about dogs to fill a text-book."

When Vicky stepped toward his dog, Mr. Lyons clasped her hand warmly as she took the leash from him.

In a lower voice, still audible to the others, he said, "Mrs. Lyons and I are disgusted at the shocking things they're printing about you, Vicky. Anyone who knows you knows what a pack of vicious lies it is. Anyone who thinks different is a fool."

"Thank you, Mr. Lyons," Vicky said huskily. Tears brimmed her eyes, and seeing them, the little man grew embarrassed. He turned to Ginny to complete the paperwork on Ramses.

Seeing that the action was over, and somewhat disappointed by the wholesome turn of events, the other customers shuffled out the door or lined up to check in.

Race drew Vicky aside and explained that he was driving into the city to see their lawyer. Eleanore had met with her lawyers; she wanted Oak Hill and was going to contest the will. Race and Vicky would need to start preparing their own case.

She went back to work in a pensive mood. They had both been extremely busy for the past two days. On both days she had come to work around dawn, left after dark and flopped into bed, alone and exhausted. She assumed Race was doing the same. She'd seen him only when they'd had business to discuss.

Their relationship was ambivalent. There was a strange kind of intimacy between them. They had exposed the most basic, primitive parts of each other's natures, and yet they had yet to learn all the background information and details that usually preceded such a discovery. Would they ever fill in those gaps? Vicky didn't know. She only knew that there was no going back on what they had done together, no point in pretending he was a stranger. He didn't know her well; yet at the same time he knew her better than anybody. There was also no point in pretending she didn't want to repeat the experience. She knew he did, too. They talked of wills and

property and expenses, but the hunger was there between
them all the time. It was in his eyes as well as hers. And yet
for two nights they had each slept alone in wide, empty
beds....

"Vicky, the plumber can't come today. His wife's having
a baby. Is tomorrow all right?" Ginny asked, interrupting
Vicky's dreaming.

Vicky laughed. "Of course! And congratulate him for
me!"

The sun was low and golden in the sky when Vicky left the
kennel and walked home. The evening was hot, but the air
smelled sweet with flowers and fresh-cut grass. Vicky sat
with Rebel on her back porch and drank a beer, occasionally pouring some of it into a saucer for Rebel, who lapped
it up eagerly. This was the life: a cold beer, a warm evening
and the loving companionship of woman's best friend.

Rebel, in her eager, nonverbal way, told Vicky of a day
spent chasing rabbits and chewing up slippers. Vicky told
her woes to Rebel, who listened, her eyes big, brown and
sympathetic. They hugged each other and sat in companionable silence for a while, sipping and lapping beer.

A dog gave love as it should be given, without reservations, criticism or threats of withdrawal, Vicky reflected. A
dog was a loyal and reliable friend. A dog was a fun and af-
fectionate companion. And if Vicky's being a source of food
played a large part in Rebel's uncritical adoration of her, if
Rebel's contributions to Vicky's life and ideas were limited,
at least Rebel had never hurt, disappointed or rejected her.
The same could be said of every dog Vicky had ever known.
It didn't apply to a single person she'd ever known.

She was pondering the compensations of a life devoted to
animals when she heard a car in the distance at Race's
house. The motor stopped and a car door slammed. Vicky
decided she would go to find out what the lawyer had said;
she ignored the compelling hunger that was her stronger
reason for walking through the woods to Race's house.
Rebel was distracted by the ducks at the river, and Vicky
approached the house alone. She walked around to the front

and found an attractive young man, about Race's age, knocking on the front door. He looked vaguely familiar. He turned and saw her standing in the garden—which was now somewhat better kept than when Race had first arrived.

"You must be Victoria Wood," he said.

She nodded.

"I'm Henry Race."

Her stomach dropped with superstitious fear, as if history were repeating itself; handsome young Henry Race was paying his first visit to the overgrown, abandoned family home, and the shy, wild girl who lived in the cottage was coming to meet him. Her breath came out in a rush and her feet came back to earth.

"Hank's oldest son?" she asked.

"His oldest *legitimate* son," the man corrected her.

"What do you want?"

"To talk. Can we go inside?"

"That's Race's house. I haven't got the key. I gave it to him."

"Race Bennett?"

"Yes."

They regarded each other warily. If only Race was here! He'd know what to say, how to deal with the situation, how to approach this man who looked so much like Hank. If the man had been a rabid dog, she could have coped. But she was at a loss with this well-dressed, well-spoken Georgetowner, who was looking at her with mingled distaste and interest.

Vicky's long red hair was loose and curling wildly in the humidity. She was wearing old clothes, which, of course, covered only the essentials. Henry Race's eyes homed in on the swell of her breasts and the smooth expanse of her belly, which both glistened with a light film of sweat.

"So you're the woman my father kept out here," Henry Race said speculatively.

"I wasn't his mistress," Vicky stated firmly.

His eyes raked her disbelievingly. "You're certainly dressed like a mistress, if a rather rustic one."

"I'm dressed like a kennel girl," she said tightly. "I know Hank had affairs, but that had nothing to do with me."

"Do you really expect me to believe that he spent all those weekends out here with a woman like you and never touched you?"

"Yes!"

"Then why did he leave you a piece of land worth a small fortune? Land, I might add, that has been in my mother's family for a century."

"He probably left it to me because I was the only one who cared about it! Or him!"

"It is by right my mother's land—"

"Hank *bought* it," she pointed out.

"—and my father had no right to leave it to his bastard son and his redheaded tart!"

Henry stepped so close that his hot breath fanned Vicky's face, and in sudden revulsion, she shoved him away with all her strength. Their mutual hostility exploded, and in pure rage, he grabbed her as if he would shake her till her head flew off.

"Take your hands off her!" Race snarled furiously behind them.

Vicky turned to see him just coming around the corner of the house.

"Race!" she cried in relief, pulling free of Henry's grip and running toward him. "Where's your car?"

"At the kennel. I was looking for you there," he said tersely. He grabbed her arm and roughly pulled her behind him as he approached the other man menacingly. "Who the hell are you?"

"Henry Race."

Race stopped dead in his tracks and stared at Henry in surprise. Vicky realized for the first time that Race had three half brothers he'd never even seen. The two men sized each other up: the pampered, blue-blooded heir to a respectable fortune, and the unwanted bastard of a young lawyer and a farm girl. What memories of rejection and envy, of taunting children and their insults, were passing through Race's mind? she wondered.

"So you're my unknown brother," murmured Henry at last.

A great calm seemed to come over Race then, the old hurts and memories going back to the past, where they belonged, the strong, resolved adult coming to the surface again. He had dealt with this years ago and made his peace with it.

"I'm not your brother. We were fathered by the same man. That's all."

Henry seemed to accept this without rancor. "You don't look a bit like him."

"You do," said Race. "But you're not much like him, are you?" Henry lacked the warmth, the easy charm, that had been so much a part of Hank.

"No. For one thing, I don't cheat on my fiancée."

Race smiled without humor, refusing to rise to the bait. "I didn't mean that, but I'll let it pass. What do you want?"

"I was hoping to make this woman see reason, but it's obviously useless—"

"It usually is," Race agreed sympathetically. Vicky shot him an evil look.

"But you seem a reasonable man," Henry continued. "My mother wants this land back. It was in her family for a century, and my father had no right to leave it to...outsiders. To avoid a lengthy lawsuit and a lot of nasty publicity—which will probably hurt you more than it will hurt us, since we, at least, are used to it—we're prepared to make a handsome cash offer and settle out of court."

"No."

"What?"

"I said no. Vicky?"

"No," said Vicky.

"There's your answer. Sorry you wasted a trip, but you should have phoned; we're in the book," Race said pleasantly.

Henry's face grew hard. "Now see here—"

"There's no point in arguing. We're happy here and we've made up our minds to stay," Race said in the same deceptively nice voice.

Anger contorted Henry's handsome features. "Yes, I can believe you're happy here, living on my father's land and sleeping with his mistress—"

Race hit Henry so hard he fell down. Henry sprawled in the grass like a rag doll. Race's whole body was tense with suppressed violence.

"Get up," he growled. Henry obeyed. He dabbed at his bleeding mouth and glared at Race but made no move to attack him—which was just as well, since Race looked ready to tear him to pieces. "Until the day you get a court order to take possession of this land, it's mine. And I'm telling you to get off and stay off. And if I ever hear you slander this woman again, I will personally rearrange your face so well that no one will ever again see the resemblance to our father."

It was a crude form of persuasion, but effective. Henry got into his car and drove off with undignified haste.

Race studied his bloodied knuckles pensively for a moment. "Have you noticed I'm starting to behave like you? I never used to do things like that."

Vicky sighed, a mixture of relief and despair. "You do realize, don't you, that this has only made things worse? They'll do their best to make us regret this."

"It was worth it though, wasn't it?" His grin was wicked.

"Since you came here I've counted on you to smooth things over and sweet-talk people. I think I may have misplaced my faith in you," she teased him.

"It's the effect you have on me. And the heat. Let's go inside."

He took her hand and led her unprotestingly into the house. He switched on the big overhead fans, and the rooms became cool and comfortable in the fading twilight.

Race opened a couple of beers and they sat in silence for a few moments, contemplating private demons. People usually baffled Vicky, but with Race she had moments of insight.

"Were you hitting him, or Hank?" she asked.

Race looked surprised for a moment, then reflected. "Both, I guess. Hank for leaving me and you in this mess the way he left me and my mom in it all those years ago. And Henry for roughing you up and insulting you."

"You rough me up and insult me all the time," she pointed out.

"You give me cause," Race said evilly. "Anyhow, I pay in my own way for that."

"It's strange to think you have brothers you don't know."

"Yeah."

There was a silence.

"Race . . . being an only child, moving around, were you lonely?" She herself had been so lonely.

"Sure. I guess I used to wonder about Hank's other kids. Would they like me? Would we play together if we were allowed to? Would I have a family then? But as I got older I knew they would resent me the way . . . the way you told me an old dog resents it when a family buys a new dog. It would never have been any good. I realized that years ago."

"I wonder what would have happened to all of us if he had married your mother," Vicky mused.

"Maybe it's just as well he didn't. She had too much self-respect to put up with a philanderer like Hank. And she got over Hank and fell in love with Wade—who's the better man, if you ask me."

"But what about you? Children can be very cruel to a kid who's different." She spoke from experience.

"That's true." Race smiled, remembering. "But a few fist fights usually settled everything and put me at the top of the heap. And I liked fighting."

"I can believe that."

"I seem to be reverting to my childhood ways since I met you."

"It's the country air," she assured him.

"Anyway, I wouldn't have fit in with what Hank wanted from his sons. Can you see me dressing in three-piece suits like Henry, pushing papers with soft white hands?"

"No," she said decisively. Her gaze drifted to where a strong, work-roughened hand rested on his thigh. There was a long scar across the back of it. She reached out to trace it lightly with her fingertips. "Where'd you get this?"

Race grinned wickedly. "I was eighteen, sawing wood at a building site when a pretty girl walked by. My eyes followed her and my hands forgot what they were doing. I scarcely even felt it when I did it. She had the most incredible—"

"Spare me the details," Vicky said dryly. Race laughed.

"And this?" he asked as his fingers traced the small, jagged marks on her arm.

"Rebel did that."

"Rebel?"

"Mm-hmm. She's such a scaredy-cat—fights with her eyes closed. Three years ago a beagle attacked her. I pulled him off, but Rebel kept snapping at the air with her eyes closed—never even knew it was me she nailed."

"Man's best friend?"

"What about this?" She traced a mark on his arm.

"I got sliced by some rusty tin. But this one's even better." He unbuttoned his shirt and showed her a mark on his shoulder. "A welder got me there."

"Another pretty girl?"

"No. He'd just become a father."

"So has our plumber, unless I miss my guess. Haven't you got any scars not associated with building sites?" she asked in disappointment.

"Your turn," he teased her.

"This is where a raccoon at the Children's Zoo bit me. The shots afterward hurt a lot more than being bitten."

"Poor Vicky." He lightly kissed the mark on her arm.

"And this—" she pointed to two small pricks on her thigh "—is where the snake in India bit me."

Race met her eyes for a long moment before he lowered his head and slowly, tenderly kissed the spot.

"Haven't you got any scars not associated with being bitten?" he whispered.

"This," she said weakly, pointing to the mark on her stomach.

"Hmm. What's this?" Race's hot lips explored the spot.

"Appendix," she said with a sigh.

Race rested his head briefly against her breasts. He slipped his hand under her half T-shirt to touch them lovingly. He raised his head and kissed her hungrily, his tongue tasting hers. They were both breathing heavily when he pulled away.

Their eyes met and held.

"Come upstairs," he whispered.

Vicky and Race stood up, their eyes never leaving each other's faces. He led her by the hand up the wide staircase, to the big bedroom, which was softly lit by a dying sun and a borning moon. The night air stirred the curtains at the window, and the overhead fan blew the breeze around the two of them, a soft whirlwind of air vainly seeking to cool the heat of their entwined bodies.

They undressed each other slowly, languidly, seeking to draw out the moments, to make the night eternal.

"And this?" she whispered.

"You were there, remember? Captain did that," he breathed against her lips. His hands roamed over her strong body. "And this?"

"Oh, that. Myron did that yesterday when he was saying hello. Joe's having... a lot of trouble...." She lost track of her thoughts as Race removed the rest of her clothes and insistently guided her hand to the fastening of his trousers.

"And this?" she whispered teasingly a few minutes later.

"I think a lot of men have one there, Vicky."

"Hmm. Does it hurt?"

He drew in a sharp breath. "It does when you do that."

"Let me kiss it and make it better," she whispered.

"You don't . . ." Whatever else Race had intended to say
was lost in the enraptured sigh that escaped him as Vicky's
tender lips explored his hard masculinity, gently and teasingly—and thoroughly enough to make his legs so weak he
sank to the bed, pulling her on top of him as he lay back on
the crisp cotton sheets.

"You're a witch," he whispered shakily. "A sweet, soft,
warm witch."

"I've been called worse things," she admitted breathlessly as his hands traveled boldly over her body, running
lightly over the smooth skin of her back, pressing into the
firm flesh of her bottom, stroking her flat stomach, caressing the silken flesh of her upper arms.

She felt they were descending together into a whirlpool of
hot sensation and burning desire, melting together into one
soul, one heart, one endless, yearning ache that promised a
rich and shattering fulfillment if they had the courage to
seek it together. Her eyes closed, and she abandoned herself to the hot pleasure coursing through her body as Race
buried his face in her luxuriant hair, caressed her trembling
thighs, moved to trace slow, burning kisses along her throat
and jaw.

His lips met hers, and their kisses were sweet, so sweet she
wanted to tell him but could find no words. She stroked his
smooth cheek and let her eyes tell him, her normally proud
expression softened by the wonder of what he was making
her feel.

"Vicky," he whispered huskily, pressing a kiss into her
palm. "Oh, Vicky, you make me hate the nights I spend
alone."

His sure hands touched her breasts, lightly at first, then
more insistently as his passion mounted and her responses
became uncontrollable. His lips and tongue teased her,
playing with her, tantalizing her, until she pulled his head to
her breasts and held him tightly, pleading with him to fulfill his silent promises.

She felt him tracing hot kisses over her flat stomach and
wide hips, then his smooth face nuzzled her thighs affec-

tionately. She twisted her hands into his wavy brown hair, reveling in its healthy texture and the way it curled around her fingers. His hands moved to part her thighs, and suddenly her whole body went rigid as she realized what he was about to do.

"Relax," Race whispered, caressing her reassuringly and squeezing one of her hands with his own. She hovered for a moment between apprehension and desire, then relaxed as their eyes met; the tenderness and passion flowing between them promised her that this would bring them both pleasure that would bind them together, pleasure devoid of shame or selfishness.

He sensed her acquiescence and lowered his head again to tenderly kiss and probe her hot feminine core, teasing and tasting, seeking and demanding, promising and fulfilling. She clutched the pillow under her head and arched her back, breathing heavily, sighing and crying out again and again as a fine sheen of perspiration covered her whole body. She rode the waves of pleasure, cresting them again and again until she feared she would actually collapse from exhaustion and begged Race to stop. He finally did, and she lay absolutely still for a few moments, awed by the sensations still coursing through her, certain that she would never again move a muscle.

Then she felt him lie on top of her, felt his mouth move roughly over her face, felt his hard body urging its way into hers, and she knew that there was something else she wanted, something else that could still move her with desire. She answered him, her body clinging to his, her movements matching his perfectly. She met his kisses as hungrily as if the evening had only just begun, and rose with him to a climax more shattering than anything that had gone before.

She lay weakly beneath him when it was over, too exhausted to mind the heat or the heaviness of his body on top of her. She felt him try to relieve her of his weight, pushing himself up on trembling arms.

"No, don't," she whispered. "Stay where you are."

"No, you'll..." He looked into her drowsy, passion-heavy eyes and changed his mind. "Okay."

"Do you mind if I sleep a bit?" she sighed.

Just before she drifted off, she thought she heard him chuckle.

Vicky awoke at first light, as usual. She was disoriented for a moment and very hot. Then sweet memories flooded in and she stretched contentedly.

Race had one arm and one leg draped across her body, which accounted for the heat. But it was a pleasant sensation and she stayed as she was. His head rested next to hers on the pillow they shared, and he was lost in the sleep of deep exhaustion. With good reason, she thought, and smiled deliciously; he had spent most of the night proving that his scars didn't disable him in the least.

She turned her head slightly to study his face, which was so vulnerable, even young, in sleep. His hair looked very dark against the white pillow, as if his halo had completely fallen off in the night. Perhaps it had; no angel should have known the things he had known about her body. Looking at him now, Vicky was almost astounded that he could look so innocent after the things he had done in the dark.

She sighed in remembered pleasure and stretched again. Race stirred sleepily, his body pressing against hers. Despite the satiation of the night, she felt her hungers awaken as he shifted more heavily onto her.

"Hey," she whispered, and nudged him. He grunted and burrowed into the pillow. "Race, wake up," she insisted.

He opened bleary, confused gray eyes. They widened slightly as he saw her an inch from his nose. He pulled back to focus slightly and then seemed to come to life.

"Good morning," he murmured. He kissed her softly and went back to sleep.

Vicky, whose own plan had been much encouraged by his kiss, tried to rouse him.

"Go away," he pleaded. "No, don't. Just hold me and be quiet."

She snuggled up to him and furthered her purpose with teasing caresses. Race tried to pretend sleep for a few minutes, but it soon became obvious he was wide awake now.

"Race," she said significantly.

He opened his eyes, his look one of mingled exhaustion, exasperation and passion. She grinned.

"Vicky, have mercy. Let me sleep just one more hour." He added sternly, "I'm not eighteen anymore."

"No. But you're holding up remarkably well."

Race rolled his eyes and sighed in defeat. "Okay. But can I please have a cup of coffee first?"

"How can you think of coffee at a moment like this?" she demanded indignantly.

Race reminded her, in graphic detail, just how unfair that question was and exactly why he needed some caffeine. She conceded his point and went downstairs in her shorts and T-shirt to make a pot of coffee.

The coffee was brewing and the windows were open to a glorious Virginia dawn as Vicky wandered into Race's makeshift office in the dining room. There were, as usual, scraps of notes and sketches all over the table. There was a very rough drawing of the kennel. She smiled as she studied it. The pillars holding up the front porch were all drawn in her image, like caryatids in an ancient Greek temple. Race was getting to be very fanciful.

She went over to his drafting board to see what he'd been working on. Her smile vanished and her whole body tensed. She leaned over and peered more closely at it, just to be sure.

It was a preliminary drawing for a house to be built on her land. There was no mistaking it: he had drawn in the lightning-struck tree and the curve in the river; it was a part of Oak Hill she knew well. It was an area on this side of the river, on the eastern boundary of the property.

He was getting ready to build. He was getting ready to close up the kennel. He was going to tear her life down around her.

Vicky didn't even remember leaving the house. She found herself running through the woods in her bare feet, run-

ning to get away from him and his strong arms and his hot
kisses, from his dreams and schemes, from what she'd just
discovered.

She finally stopped in exhaustion, gasping for breath, and
flung herself down onto the soft grass in the shade of an oak
tree. She cried and held herself, wanting to lick her wounds
the way Rebel did.

She knew why he had come. She had always known; he
had never made any secret of it. He wanted Oak Hill for
himself. For himself! He didn't give a damn about the kennel. He only wanted the land! They had united forces
against Eleanore, and she had been foolish enough to forget they were still enemies. Last night she had gone into his
arms the way a river flows to the sea. And he was going to
take away everything she had worked for and destroy the
only place she'd ever belonged!

Why him? Why him? Why had she done it? She pounded
the ground with her fists, sobbing with hurt and disappointment and fear. She burrowed into the grass like an animal seeking shelter, willing the earth to absorb her, body
and soul.

Much later, when her tears and rage were finally spent,
she repeated the question more calmly: why him? And the
answer came with strong, unshakable certainty, filling her
with sickening dread.

She was in love with him.

She rolled over and stared at the overhead branches. She
was in love. She, who had shut men out of her life as an un-
satisfactory waste of time and energy, was head over heels
in love. It would be ironic, if it weren't so disastrous. She
had rejected Dean, an animal lover like her, who would have
backed up her work and her commitment to it till his dying
day; Dean, who would have cared for her honestly and sin-
cerely. She had dropped other men in her past for the
slightest offense, the slightest infringement.

And now she was in love with a man who couldn't tell a
yellow Labrador from a golden retriever; the charming,
clever son of a notorious philanderer; a man who had

proven beyond a doubt that he was an experienced ladies' man and who, far from supporting her work, wanted to bulldoze it around her ears.

How could she possibly be in love with him? But she knew. She knew. She had known it for a while. It lived in every moment between them: in the savage, tender fire of his touch, in their easy laughter, in the quick, sure way they talked, in the silent communication of their eyes.

There would be no happy endings now. If he won, he'd take everything away from her. And if she won, he'd go back to California and leave a void in her life that nothing would ever fill. She had grown too used to his quiet strength in times of trouble, to his clever charm smoothing over the rough edges of her life, to his teasing, to his laughter, to his passion.... He had come on the last breath of spring and made himself a part of her heart before summer's heat was over.

But she would never forgive him if he destroyed Oak Hill. She would get over it; she would find other work and another home. But she would never forgive him for making her vulnerable and then betraying her like this.

And she would never again go into his embrace as if he himself were her home.

She was grim and subdued as she began work early that morning. She figured Race would have fallen back into his unconscious state when the coffee didn't materialize, so she could count on a few hours to pull herself together before he appeared.

Brian noticed her set face and terse voice and attributed it to all the "gapers" that had been bothering her. He gallantly offered to clobber anyone who pestered her too much.

"Just say the word, Vic, and he's a dead man!" He smacked his fist resoundingly into the palm of the opposite hand to make his point.

Beside herself with misery, loving Brian in an exasperated way and grateful for his teasing affections, Vicky kissed his cheek. He caught the pained look in her eyes before she lowered them.

"Hey, man, what ails you?"

She shook her head. Brian watched her in awkward silence for a moment. Then he squeezed her hand warmly. His voice, however, had its usual teasing note when he spoke.

"Just remember, I'm of age now if you ever change your mind about me."

Joe Hanley was working morosely with Myron.

"He sits; he stays; he heels; he just can't seem to understand that he's almost two hundred pounds too heavy to be a lapdog."

"So I see," said Vicky as Myron pinned her to the wall and washed her face. "What do you—"

There was a sudden explosion outside, so loud they heard it over the barking and the piped-in music. Then Brian and Rebecca and Ginny were all shouting. Vicky ran to the far left wing. As soon as she entered it she saw water everywhere, gushing from burst pipes, flooding the wing and drenching her staff.

She ran outside and shut off the water pressure for the whole kennel. Then she went back inside and surveyed the wreckage. This was the limit.

"Get the plumber out here right now! I don't care if you have to drag him kicking and screaming out of the maternity ward!"

Nine

Race didn't show up till lunchtime. If he had intended to ask Vicky why she had disappeared that morning, one look at her haggard, distressed expression told him this wasn't the moment to discuss personal questions.

"What's wrong?" he asked as soon as he saw her.

She wordlessly showed him the wreckage in the far left wing: burst pipes, flooding and the plumber and his brother-in-law taking everything apart as they repaired the system. Race let out a low whistle.

"What a mess," he said softly.

Vicky's expression was grim. Race stroked her hair to comfort her. She jerked her head away and stalked off to the big sink in the back hall, where she started washing food bowls. The plumbers had restored the water pressure to all wings except the damaged one. Vicky had called up everyone who had the day off and asked them to come in for a few hours; they had been unable to get any work done without water that morning and would need extra help to get it all done now. She had not called Race. She would cut her tongue out before she would ever ask him for help again.

Race came to stand by the sink and watch her speculatively while she worked. She heaved a big pile of dirty food bowls into soapy water, scrubbed them viciously and then transferred them into clear water for rinsing. She did not look at Race. She was certain this was in some way his fault. If she had not been dallying with him in the twilight, she would have thought to come over and turn off the water pressure and this would not have happened. And if that was hysterically unfair and unrealistic, tough.

"What are you thinking, Vicky?" Race asked in a low voice, aware that something besides faulty plumbing was giving her that pained, angry look.

"I'm thinking this makes it all rather nice for you, doesn't it?"

His eyes narrowed. "What's that supposed to mean?"

She stopped working and faced him with haunted, accusing eyes. Her voice was dead and flat when she spoke. "The plumber says the real problem is underground, in the water main to that wing. When he's done repairing the mess in here, he's going to have to break ground to fix that. It's going to take over a week and cost a fortune. And I'll have to close down that wing and turn customers away, since I can't operate without a water supply. So I'm losing twenty-five percent of my income and laying out almost every penny I've banked this summer for repairs. All of which means that unless a miracle occurs or money drops from heaven . . . you win." That last came out in a husky undertone.

"Vicky, don't worry about that—"

"Don't *worry* about it? I never think of anything else!"

"Don't you? Well, I do. What about us?"

"Us? Us! There is no us!" she snapped. "One wins and one loses. And if I lose, I'm not sticking around to watch you bulldoze my kennel or turn it into a country club!"

Race closed his eyes and tried without success to regain his patience. He gave up the effort and told her tersely that the question of who won and who lost was probably academic at that point, since their lawyer had called to say things looked very bad and he was going into the city again to meet with her.

"What's wrong?" she asked in alarm.

"I don't know yet! But if you're so convinced the kennel's going to go bust anyhow, I wouldn't worry about it if I were you, since it's obvious that what happens to me and to the rest of Oak Hill is of no concern to you! Just go back to tending your dogs, Vicky!" he said nastily, and stormed out the door.

Vicky held her head in her soapy hands and tried not to cry.

"Vicky, you'd better come quick!" called Rebecca. "There's a dog back here who doesn't look so good. I think he's having some kind of fit!"

Vicky sighed. "It never rains, but it pours."

The dog was indeed having an epileptic fit, despite regular dosing with his medicine. Vicky held him still, and tried to soothe him when it was over. Then she ordered Brian to take him over to Dean Alexander's clinic to let the vet have a good look at him, just to be safe.

The day was especially long and hard. There was no water in the far left wing, but it was full of dogs; although Vicky would close down the wing the following Monday and turn customers away, she could hardly turn her boarders out into the street in the meantime, and they had to be looked after. She went out and bought more hoses, which they hooked up together to make one extra-long hose. Then they attached it to the pipes in the next-door wing, trailed it through the connecting aisles and used it to clean the runs. The process was slow, but it worked. Rebecca cleaned and refilled all fifty of the wing's water buckets by carrying them inside to the big sink and then back to the runs again. By the end of the day she had developed biceps to rival Vicky's. Désirée took any dog who looked hot or bored into Nadine's room for a quick shower. Brian watched wistfully. Until Vicky reminded him tersely of Désirée's father and his double-barreled shotgun.

The staff worked well and hard; Vicky was enormously proud of them. Even Rebecca, who had given up a day at Virginia Beach with her boyfriend, slogged water cheerfully and, like the others, volunteered to work late. Désirée by now had the full attention and admiration of the plumber's unmarried brother-in-law. As soon as feedings and afternoon cleanings were done, Vicky sent the girl home to avoid further trouble. By early evening the situation was well under control. Vicky decided to include a cash bonus in everyone's pay envelope that week. They deserved it. And besides, there seemed little point in trying to save money anymore.

Vicky was administering medications to various boarders when Dean appeared. He, too, looked haggard and tired. It was turning into a long, hot summer for all of them. She finished her work and poured them both a glass of iced tea. They sat together in the lounge.

"Brian told me about the pipes bursting when he brought in that epileptic today," Dean said.

"How's the dog?"

"He's all right. You can have him back in the morning, if you want."

"Good."

"I came to see if I could help you."

She smiled warmly at him. "That's...typical of you, Dean. But the kids have been terrific and everything's under control. So unless you feel compelled to slog fifty buckets of water at dawn, I wouldn't worry about it."

"If you've got to break ground to repair the main, that's going to cost a fortune."

"Yes."

"How's this going to affect your agreement with Race?"

"It means I can't possibly get by without using the capital Hank left. Which means Race has proved his point and he wins," she said tiredly.

"Not necessarily," said Dean.

"What do you mean?"

"I could help you."

She met his eyes steadily. "We're talking about a lot of money, Dean."

"I know."

"A loan?"

"Yes."

Vicky knew he came from a wealthy family. He certainly had enough to keep her going until she could recover from this most recent disaster. She could get Race off her back, take care of her bills, and pay Dean back slowly. Everything might just work out. All she had to do was take advantage of Dean....

"Why are you doing this?" she asked.

"You know why."

"Dean, I can't let you do this—lay out that kind of money for personal reasons that aren't...that won't...that I can't..." She stopped in confusion. There was no kind way of telling him that even if she wasn't already in love with another man, she could never love him.

"I'm not trying to buy your affection, Vicky," he said gently.

"I know."

"I just want to help you." On a less personal note, "Anyhow, this really is the best kennel around, and as a vet I'd like to see it stay open."

"I don't know," she said in guilty confusion. It didn't seem fair to Dean. It didn't seem fair to Race. Though why she should worry about being fair to Race was quite beyond her.

"Just think it over, Vicky. The offer remains open. I don't expect anything in return. I think I've already guessed that another man has what I want most."

"No!" she said hotly. "He doesn't. I couldn't. Not—not the way things are...."

"We don't always want what it's sensible for us to want," Dean said softly.

"Now you sound like Joe Hanley," she said ruefully. "Doling out bits of country wisdom."

He was about to respond when Race entered the room. If he was surprised to see Dean, he hid it well. But he had obviously decided to change tactics in dealing with the vet.

"Hi, Dean. It's good to see you."

"It is? I mean, it is. Hi, Race."

Race stuck out his hand for a friendly handshake, and Dean took it without hesitation.

Before they could say anything more, Myron came bounding into the room and threw his whole body gleefully at the three of them. Race and Vicky leaped out of his path, and all two hundred pounds of him went flying into Dean. Dean fell over backward. Vicky and Race tried to pick him up while Myron bounded around the room, whoofing merrily.

Joe came into the room, looking mournful. "Sorry, Doc."

Dean waved a hand. He was still too winded to speak.

Joe shook his head slowly. "We worked for half an hour. He was a real gentleman, did everything perfectly. As soon as I told him to relax…well, you can see for yourselves what happened." He shook his head again and sat down. Myron came over and slobbered on him.

"Rebecca!" Vicky called. Rebecca appeared in the doorway. "Will you please take Myron back to his run? I think Joe's had about all he can take today."

Rebecca grinned knowingly and did as she was asked— with some difficulty, since Myron didn't want to break up the party.

Vicky poured iced tea for the two newcomers and they all chatted together in the lounge, tired and hot.

Joe studied Race for a moment before saying, "You look troubled, son. More bad news?"

Race shifted uneasily and glanced at Vicky. He had everyone's full attention now.

"What did you find out?" she asked, a dreadful foreboding taking hold of her.

"It looks like Eleanore's got a better case than we thought, Vicky," he said slowly.

"What do you mean?"

His eyes met her gently, sadly, wishing he didn't have to tell her this. "It seems that the contract Hank signed with Eleanore's father stipulated that Hank would leave the land to her if he predeceased her."

Vicky's stomach dropped, her mouth fell open and her vision clouded as she plopped into a chair. Her mouth worked, but no words would come.

Race's eyes were pained as he took in her stricken expression. "I'm sorry, Vicky."

"But, Race," Dean insisted, "surely something can be done. That was thirty-five years ago. Eleanore never lived here, but you were born here and Vicky's lived here for the past three years. You're his son, for God's sake!"

"Our lawyer says we can certainly get a cash settlement," said Race without interest. "But we haven't a hope in hell of keeping the land."

"But how could Hank have agreed to that?" asked Joe.

"Evidently he only paid a piddling sum for it. The idea was that it was to be for Eleanore and their kids. I suppose they didn't foresee how rich Hank would become or how much he would come to own in time. And he didn't foresee... all the things that would happen here."

"But how could he have left it to you and Vicky, in that case?" demanded Dean. "He was a lawyer himself! He must have known what would happen!"

"Sentimental gesture," Vicky said huskily, and met Race's eyes.

"Yes," Race said. "And maybe he thought he could get away with it. His wife and kids didn't give a damn about this place, and evidently Eleanore never even knew the terms of her father's deal with Hank. Her lawyers only noticed it when they began preparing the case against us. Eleanore would normally never have risked the scandal of suing us. But now that the media's made a scandal anyhow, she's got nothing to lose. Maybe she even thinks she can win back a part of her self-respect by getting rid of me and Vicky for good."

Everyone was silent. And what was there to say, after all? Eleanore would take over the land, close down the kennel

and let it all go back to the derelict and overgrown ruin it
had been three years ago. All Vicky's plans, Race's dreams
and their stormy arguments would fade into the past. All
that longing and effort for nothing; everything either of
them had wanted would be lost in the Virginia creeping vine,
the tall grass and the summer mist.

Brian came in to tell her they were running low on sanitizer; she should order more next week. Vicky nodded. She
probably wouldn't bother. If Eleanore moved fast, they
would be closing down soon, probably before summer's
end. It was over.

There being nothing else to say, Joe asked the vet for a lift
home. Vicky would want to cry in private. Joe put a hand
on her shoulder and squeezed it to give her courage. Dean
touched her arm lightly and told her to call if she needed
anything; his offer was still open, if it would help at all.

"What offer?" Race asked Vicky after the two men had
left.

"It doesn't matter now," she mumbled.

"Vicky—"

"Please, Race, I can't talk right now."

"I don't want to leave you alone."

"I'll be... I need..." Without another word she fled from
the room, leaving Race behind in brooding silence.

Nearly blinded by her own tears, she ran down the familiar path, past her cottage, through the woods and along the
river until she reached her favorite spot in the shadow of a
big tree at the wildest part of the river. The sun was low and
round, streaking the sky with amber and violet as Vicky sat
down, breathless and trembling.

She sat in a little huddled ball, holding her knees and
rocking back and forth as she sobbed. She held herself
tighter, trying to lock out the pain and despair. She didn't
know how long she sat there, sobbing brokenly and trying
to master her thoughts and fears, but the sun was disap-
pearing on the horizon when she felt another presence behind her. She didn't even need to open her eyes to know it
was Race.

Wordlessly he sat down behind her and wrapped his arms and legs around her, as if to ward off pain and dread in the same way she had tried to do it. Slowly the warmth and comfort of his reassuring strength penetrated her pain-racked consciousness. The tears stopped flowing and she rubbed her face on her knees to dry it. She sat huddled in his embrace like an animal, mindlessly absorbing his calm and confidence. She rubbed her head against his arm. His other hand released his grip on her to come up and stroke her tumbled hair. Vicky tilted her head back against his shoulder, eyes closed, and sighed while he petted her like a wounded deer.

Race's hands kneaded her aching shoulders and tired arms, smoothed over the swell of her breasts, then down her stomach as it moved in and out to the deep steady rhythm of her breathing. He stroked and caressed her legs, spreading warmth throughout her body.

She didn't know when it happened, but at some point the nature of his touch changed and so did her response to it. The hands that moved over her body with such familiarity now sought to awaken her more than to comfort her. Vicky gave herself up to their sensual coaxing, seeking forgetfulness in the magic of Race's touch.

She tilted her head so his hot lips could seek out her neck and cheek, taste the warm skin of her shoulder, trace the delicate shape of her ear.

He touched her as if he owned her now, and when he unhesitatingly pushed her shorts off her hips, Vicky gave a low moan of satisfaction. She struggled to help him pull her T-shirt over her head, then lay back in his embrace again, willing him to do whatever he wanted with her to chase her demons away.

With one hand he teased her naked breasts while he slid the other across her stomach and over her abdomen to rest on the soft hair between her legs. Vicky gripped his thighs with her hands, pressed her back more firmly against his hard chest and pushed her hips forward, encouraging the pressure of his questing hand. He obliged her by rubbing the area with gentle firmness. Vicky moaned deep in her throat, a primitive sound of mingled anticipation and pleasure. She had forgotten everything now, everything except what Race was doing to her in this moment.

Race deepened his exploration of her feminine core, teasing her, promising her, entrancing her. No one had ever touched her like this, and the dark, intimate sensuality of it overwhelmed her. She writhed in his embrace, moaned pleadingly, rubbed his thigh in answer to his teasing rhythm, moved her hips against his hand, seeking to increase his pressure and her pleasure.

Race was talking to her, burning sensual whispers meant to encourage her wildness, to set her free, to stir her imagination. Vicky answered him in a low, throbbing voice, demanding, insisting, pleading, scarcely understanding what she was saying.

She arched sensuously when the moment came, pressing her hand over his, throwing her head back in abandon as she absorbed the incredible sensations tearing through her body. She heard Race's low, encouraging murmurs as if from a distance and scarcely knew that the wild, strangled cries she heard were coming from her own throat.

When it was over, she sagged against him weakly, spent. A warm feeling of contentment flooded her body and she savored it. Her lips curved into a soft smile as she felt Race kissing her hair.

"Thank you," she whispered.

"My pleasure." He sounded amused.

Vicky suddenly remembered they both had good cause not to be amused at anything right now. She willfully shoved the thought away, not ready to return to the world yet. And Race? Had he found any forgetfulness in giving it to her?

She shifted and turned around to meet his eyes. They were warm and tender, a dark deep gray. She smiled at him. He smiled back, but his face was still strained with the cares and the worries of the day. The least she could do, she thought nobly, was to give him some forgetfulness, too. Her eyes raked him.

"Why are you still dressed?" she asked wickedly.

His eyes grew smoky. "I'm waiting for you to do something about that," he answered huskily.

Her eyes burned into his as she unbuttoned his shirt and slipped it off his shoulders. She laid her hand on a strategic part of his trousers. Race drew in a deep breath.

"You must be getting uncomfortable," she teased him. He nodded. "Well, we'll see what we can do about that." She unfastened his trousers and pulled them off his body. "Care for a swim?"

"Come here," he growled.

She did. She lay in his arms and smoothed his tired face with gentle fingers. His eyes looked restless and uncertain, quite at odds with the insistent pressure of his body against hers.

"What are you thinking?" she whispered.

"That I want you to make love to me. As if you mean it. As if nothing else matters," he answered in a low, longing voice.

Surprised and aroused at his urgency, she did as he asked with no thought but to please him. They rolled over together in the soft grass, their bodies touched by the summer breeze, their whispers echoed by the lapping water. They caressed each other with exquisite tenderness, kissed each other with obsessive intent, pleasured each other without restraint or inhibitions. Race's vulnerable sighs enraptured Vicky, reaching deep into her soul, teaching her womanly instincts exactly what he needed from her.

She pushed him firmly onto his back and rose above him purposefully. His strong hands lifted her hips to assist her, and their eyes held as their bodies joined. She leaned forward, her red hair making a dark, shimmering curtain around their faces in the soft light of the rising moon.

They exchanged a long, sweet kiss, their tongues touching and mating, a premonition of what their bodies were about to do together. Vicky pressed soft kisses across his strong, impassioned face. He moved his hands insistently on her hips, urging her on. She resisted as long as she could, drawing out the sweet anticipation. Sheltered within the dark curtain of her hair, they looked into each other's eyes as she finally gave in to his urgent demand and moved against him. Their eyes held fiercely as the pleasure grew between them and their breath came in harsh, ragged gasps. Race thrust upward with unexpected violence, and Vicky dropped her head to his chest, squeezing her eyes shut with hot pleasure and crying out. Their arms tightened around each other and they mated with savage purpose, forgetting everything but the primitive rhythm between them and their mutual goal. Their pleasure crescendoed to an unbearable pitch, and they cried out as it burst within them and flung them aloft to drift back down, after many minutes, to the hard earth beneath them and the soft night air around them.

The exertion of the past hour, added to a long day preceded by an almost sleepless night, took its toll on them. Still locked in each other's arms, they fell into a deep, dreamless slumber almost immediately.

Vicky awoke first. How long had they slept? The night was dark now, the moon sitting high and full in the sky. She lay with her head pillowed on Race's shoulder. With gentle fingers she traced the curve and swell of the muscles of his chest. Would there ever be another night like this?

"What are you thinking?" he whispered.

She raised her head. "I thought you were asleep."

"Your elbow is digging into my stomach," he pointed out by way of explanation.

"Oh, sorry." She moved her arm. He settled her more comfortably against him.

"What are you thinking about?" he repeated.

"I'm wondering where you learned everything you know about women."

She felt him smile against her hair. "I'm thirty-four years old, Vicky. I picked up a few things along the way."

"Is there a woman waiting for you back there?"

"California? No, of course not." He pulled away and frowned at her. "I wouldn't be here now with you if there were."

"No, I guess not." She didn't believe he took after Hank in that way. "But there must have been someone."

"They're all in the past," he said without regret.

"And your lawyer friend?"

He smiled again. "She's happily married, Vicky. And in college we were just buddies." He paused. "And you?"

"No. No one."

"What about our friendly neighborhood vet?"

"Dean? No."

"Why is it then that he's got his hands on you every time I see him?" Race persisted.

"He was just comforting me. There was nothing else in it."

"Don't tell me he was just comforting you the night of the storm; I won't believe you."

She smiled sadly. "No. Actually, I was just comforting him in a sense. Telling him I couldn't return his, um . . ."

"Admiration?" Race supplied.

"Something like that. But he's been so kind to me ever since. I can't think why."

"Can't you? Didn't it occur to you that you don't have to please him for him to care about you? That he could just want to be kind to make you happy?"

She fell into a thoughtful silence. It was a difficult concept, that someone could love her without a list of reasons and give to her without expecting anything in return. Race followed her thoughts like a mind reader. His encircling arm squeezed her to get her attention.

"You expect it of a dog, Vicky. Hasn't it ever occurred to you to expect it from people, too?"

"No."

"And yet Hank brought you out here and set you up for nothing, when he didn't need the investment or the hassle."

"Yes . . ."

Race let her ponder it by herself this time. Much later, when their mood had lightened and they were looking at the stars, he said teasingly, "You still haven't told me where you learned everything you know about men."

"I don't know anything about men."

"After what you did to me tonight? And this morning? And last night? No wonder I'm so tired."

"You inspired me," she said extravagantly.

"Mmm. I'm glad."

"I hardly have anything to do with men, Race. I was a gawky, skinny teenager, and no one ever paid any attention to me."

"But you grew up."

"I told you I do better with animals than with people. I never felt comfortable dating men. I never knew how to act or what to say. I could never let myself go when they touched me. I guess that's a big part of the reason I'm so dedicated to work; I always knew I'd never fall in love."

Race looked surprised. "Never? That's a long time to be alone."

Vicky shrugged. And when he went back to California, it would be forever. She would never again know that wildness, that joy. A bitter hurt started to creep through her.

"Vicky," Race said hesitantly, as if sensing her withdrawal, "last night and tonight have been wonderful, like something out of time and space. But you can only take me to the stars when we're alone like this. The rest of the time we'll have to live in the real world. So I think it's time—" he took a deep breath before continuing "—to think about the future."

Here it comes, she thought. She sat up and moved away from him, avoiding the hand he reached out to her, and started pulling on her clothes. However sweet the moments, this had been another mistake. Race sat watching her.

"Vicky, don't you think we ought to renegotiate our agreement?"

"I don't see any point in it," she said stiffly.

"No point? Vicky, we were total strangers when we made that deal. Things have changed so much since then. We didn't know this would happen between us."

"No, we didn't. But there's no need to 'renegotiate,' because I'm not going to let it happen again!"

He went very still. His naked body gleamed like polished bronze in the moonlight. The dark night hid his expression. "Why?"

"Because I'm not going to let sex interfere with what's important in my life!"

"And what's important in your life, Vicky?" His tone was deadly; she was glad she couldn't see his face.

"I saw the drawings," she said steadily.

"What drawings?"

"The ones on your drafting board. Did you honestly think that taking me to bed this summer would make up for closing down my business this fall?"

"Put that crudely, no. But isn't what happens between us more important than what happens to the kennel?"

"You *will* not understand, will you? Nothing—*nothing*—matters to me more than that kennel. It's the only place I've ever belonged, it's the only real purpose I've ever had, it's the only home I've ever known."

"And your pets are the only ones who've ever loved you. Is that it?"

"Yes," she said tightly, holding back the tears. She would not let him make her cry again.

He let out a long, pained, exasperated sigh. "What you want isn't love, Vicky. It's uncritical adoration from an unthinking source. That's got nothing to do with real love. I feel sorry for you."

"I don't want you feeling sorry for me," she hissed angrily.

He pulled on his clothes as he spoke. "Well, that's tough. Because I feel the way I feel and I do what I want to do, and I'm not going to enroll in obedience classes or be satisfied with something extra in my food bowl." He stood with his hands on his hips and looked at her, his face obscured by the shadows. "I guess you really do prefer coming home to a dog at the end of the day. I thought I could make you want a man instead. For once I have to agree with Wade: I'm an arrogant fool." He turned and walked off into the night before she could agree.

Vicky went home, crying, fuming and raging. How *dare* he imply that she didn't want love? How *dare* he try to pretend his plans to destroy her life were of secondary importance? How *dare* he ridicule her values and loyalties? All very well and good for him—maybe Hank had rejected him, but Race had a mother, a grandfather and a stepfather who had all loved him, and she had had no one to love her except a pack of stray dogs wherever she went. It was easy for him to talk about coming home at night to someone when he obviously had a string of "someones" behind him. But her recent experience with Dean proved she was as hopelessly inadequate at dealing with men as she had ever been.

And now there had been Race, and she would never want anyone else again....

She hurled a lamp against the wall and it shattered into a dozen pieces. Rebel yelped and scuttled under the kitchen table. Vicky threw herself onto the sofa and howled with hurt and rage and confusion. She wished she'd never met him!

Before long she felt a cold, wet nose pressing against her neck. She looked up into Rebel's concerned brown eyes. Rebel washed her tearstained face with a gentle pink tongue and whined softly.

"Oh, Rebel, Rebel," Vicky sobbed and threw her arms around the dog. Her grip was tight enough to hurt, but Rebel didn't complain.

Vicky didn't see Race again for several days, not even from a distance. His car was gone most of the time. She didn't know where he went.

They checked out dozens of dogs at the kennel and began closing down the dry wing. The plumber showed up with a huge earth-moving machine and started digging down to the water main. There was nearly a serious accident when Désirée walked by while the plumber's brother-in-law was at the controls. Vicky sternly ordered Désirée to stay inside the building for the rest of the day and advised the plumber to get blinkers for his young assistant.

Vicky went about her work as usual, but her Trojan-like strength seemed to be failing her at last. Everything was slipping through her fingers: her kennel, her home, the only man she'd ever wanted—even her dog. Rebel had been rushed to the veterinary clinic that morning. In her infamous adventures she'd finally eaten something that didn't agree with her. She'd been taken to the vet with a high temperature, glazed eyes and severe nausea. Dean assured her

Rebel would live, but he insisted on keeping the dog at the clinic for several days after her stomach had been pumped.

Vicky couldn't summon interest in anything. She apathetically ignored Désirée and Rebecca when they tried to draw her into a water fight on Tuesday. On Wednesday she merely nodded when the plumber informed her the work would be done sooner than expected and cost less than estimated. On Thursday Brian, who had prepared a detailed, melodramatic speech explaining why he needed money for new tractor parts, was astonished when she handed him the cash without comment.

"Vicky, man, what's eating you?"

"Nothing."

"You're, like, not yourself," he insisted. "Is it Race?"

Vicky sparked for the first time in days. "Why does it always have to be Race anytime something's wrong with me?" she flared. "Couldn't it be Rebel or the plumbing or children starving in Asia? Why does everyone always assume he's the only thing on my mind?"

"I take it back," said Brian, and left as quickly as possible.

She sighed. Poor Brian. She shouldn't have yelled at him like that.

"Vicky, get a load of this," said Ginny as she passed.

"What?"

"It's a telephone message for Race. Guess who it's from."

"I don't care," Vicky said irritably. Then, before she could stop herself, she asked, "Who?"

"Eleanore Race."

"What? What did she say?"

"She thanked him for *another* lovely evening. She's changed her mind and she's willing to discuss his ideas. Would he like to come to the house for lunch tomorrow?" said Ginny. "That's all. I'll go slip it under his front door. He's never around these days. What do you suppose he's up to?" She left the building, muttering to herself.

"What indeed?" asked Vicky.

So Race had been making overtures to Eleanore. And quite successfully, from the sound of it.

Just what on earth *was* he up to now?

Ten

This will solve all our problems," said Brian proudly.

"With the tractor?" Vicky asked.

He nodded.

"How much did it cost?"

He told her.

"Brian! You spent that much on this—this—this—" she sputtered futilely as she pointed to the small, unimpressive-looking gadget resting in the palm of Brian's hand.

"Ah, now you're looking more like your old self."

"That tractor had better eat more grass than a herd of wild mustangs," she warned him, "or I'm going to use it on your hair."

Brian clutched his yellow mop defensively. "Don't worry, man. It's worth it. I've got it licked this time. I'm sure."

"Let's hope you're not barking up the wrong tree."

"Have you noticed you're starting to talk like Race?"

Vicky glared at him.

"You're a bit short-tempered these days, Vic. You should get more rest." Brian grinned evilly.

He left the building with undue haste to go and work on his beloved tractor. She peeked out the window and saw Rebel, now quite recovered from her adventures, tagging along behind him.

"Talking like Race?" she repeated.

Ironic that it should only be noticeable now that she scarcely spoke with him, scarcely saw him around. In the week since their fight at the river he had been absent every day and most evenings. And if the sight of the lights burning in his house late at night only deepened the pain of her solitary, sleepless nocturnal strolls, it was still a welcome sight; he was still at Oak Hill, even if he was a stranger again.

But how much longer would he be here? She had left the legal details to him, since he correctly assumed she'd only insult and offend Eleanore's lawyers. She didn't know how soon Eleanore would take possession of the land, how soon she herself would have to close down the kennel. Shouldn't she start warning her customers? She'd already told the staff to look for new jobs, written them references and promised them severance pay out of any money she had left over.

She had taxed Race with this question, wanting to know what to expect. He had replied vaguely that he'd let her know. She should keep everything operating as usual in the meantime, even open up the far left wing, which had remained shut despite completed repairs. He had also remarked, with the impersonal concern of a doctor, that she didn't look well and should get more rest.

Rest? How could she rest? She was losing both Oak Hill and Race. She didn't know which hurt more.

Would Race go back to California now, to the stepfather who loved him, to the business he'd built up, to those brown rocky hills and days of dry heat? Would he find a tanned, slim, well-dressed California woman who knew what to say and which fork to use, a woman who would make him forget the tall, temperamental, naive redhead he had fought with and made love with one sultry summer at Oak Hill? Vicky closed her eyes in pain.

And what about her? She'd expected to spend the rest of her life at Oak Hill, to watch the overgrown land prosper, to see the kennel's reputation grow, to do a job she loved in a place she loved. She and Hank had shared another ambition, one she'd never even told Race about. When the kennel became established and profitable enough, they had wanted to turn one whole wing into a home for stray dogs, where they would be kept without threat of destruction until Vicky could find homes for them. Now none of it would ever bear fruit.

And worse yet, for days now Vicky had been tortured by images of children running across the green hills and through the oak groves, laughing as they dived into the river and splashed one another. Her children; some with fiery red hair, and others looking like small wicked angels with dark golden halos....

She shot out of her chair and went to the back of the kennel, looking for work to do—hard, punishing, physical work.

The worst thing she could think of was the job she had once punished Désirée with: washing down the walls and floors with flea-and-tick dip. She went about this taxing, smelly, tedious job with a vengeance, working with such a frenzy that her body gleamed with sweat.

So what *would* she do now? She was back at square one, where she'd been three years ago. Dean had already offered her a job. But she couldn't take charity—and it *was* charity, since she was not in any way qualified to work in a clinic. Anyhow, now that she knew how painful unrequited love was, Vicky couldn't torment him by hanging around his place all day every day.

The best thing would be to go back to graduate school. She didn't relish the thought of more studying, but it would enable her to find more rewarding work. It was already too late to apply for this fall. She would work to save money and apply next year.

"Come on, Vicky. It's not that bad. At least you've got a vocation, right?" she chided herself.

She could eventually work in a zoo, maybe even go out to San Diego.... No, she would never go out to California and risk bumping into Race again. Well, perhaps she would open another kennel again someday, under better circumstances.

"Just find out who really owns the land first, Vicky, and make sure your partner's in good health," she muttered.

She had worked herself into a fine, messy, smelly state in the hot afternoon when Ginny called her over the intercom with some urgency. Vicky went to the front of the kennel, feeling almost lighthearted; for once she didn't care what the problem was. She was going out of business soon and wouldn't have to deal with it anymore. It occurred to her that the fumes might have affected her brain.

"Would you get a load of this?" said Ginny.

Vicky looked out the window. A stretch limousine was parked in front of the kennel. The chauffeur and Joe Hanley were helping a woman rise from her prostrate position on the pavement. Myron, suitably reprimanded for his enthusiasm, was held in Rebecca's firm grip a few yards away. Joe seemed to be apologizing profusely as he helped dust the woman off. She reassured him, evidently told the chauffeur to wait for her there and walked to the front door, patting her ice-blond hair.

Vicky froze. "Oh, my God. It's Eleanore!" she gasped.

"What?" Ginny nearly shrieked.

"Oh, no! Myron, I could kill you! Aren't things bad enough as it is? She'll nail me to the wall for this," Vicky groaned.

"She has some *nerve* if you ask me, coming here like this. I'd like to take her apart piece by piece." And Ginny was still tough enough to do it, too, Vicky knew.

Eleanore came through the front door. Her ice-blue eyes rested on the two tense women. Ginny nudged Vicky.

"It's all right, Ginny. I'll handle it," said Vicky with more confidence than she felt. She spoke to Eleanore. "Why don't you come into the lounge?"

Eleanore nodded regally, followed Vicky to the lounge and chose to sit in the only straight-backed chair in the room. She took in Vicky's long, strong, well-shaped and scantily clad body gleaming with sweat, the fair skin with a sprinkling of freckles across the nose, the wild red hair and the apprehensive green eyes.

"So you're Vicky," she said in her cool, cultured voice. A slight smile curved her mouth. "You are quite unmistakably the woman Henry described to me."

"I—I'm sorry I was so nasty to him," Vicky said haltingly. "He said some awful things that made me lose my temper."

"Henry conceded that he might have been rather rude to you. Please allow me to apologize for him," Eleanore said politely.

"Well . . . welcome to Oak Hill," Vicky said after an uncomfortable silence. "It's too bad you didn't come before. Hank . . . Hank was very proud of this kennel."

"Yes. I believe he was. But my husband had many projects, and this one was outside my realm of experience."

"They why are you here today?" Vicky challenged her.

"Because now that Hank is gone, this property and your claim to it have become my direct concern." She added with distaste, "And the media have made me wish to see this entire matter concluded as soon as possible."

Vicky met Eleanore's eyes with a level gaze. "I can't stop you from taking Oak Hill away from me, and I can't prove to the media that they're wrong about me, but I'm telling you honestly as one woman to another that there was nothing between me and Hank. I was never his mistress."

"I know."

"You do?" Vicky asked in astonishment.

"I do now. I was, I admit, hard to convince."

"How did . . . Oh. Race talked to you," Vicky guessed.

"Yes." Something like admiration warmed her expression. "He's a very persuasive young man. He also has no illusions about my late husband, for better or worse, and is one of the few people who has spoken to me honestly about Hank since his death."

"And that convinced you?"

"That, and the things he said about you, Vicky. He's a good judge of character, as Hank was; he continued to insist that you were strictly a good friend and business associate of Hank's, and I came to believe him." A glimmer of amusement shone in her eyes as she glanced at Vicky's attire. "Although I must say that if you parade around dressed like that in front of reporters, you must expect misunderstandings to arise."

Vicky shifted uncomfortably. "Well . . . I suppose so. But Hank never saw me that way. He was like a father to me, and I loved him."

"Would you believe I loved him, too?"

Vicky didn't, and she knew it showed in her eyes.

"If you will forgive me for saying so, Vicky, you're still very young and perhaps rather naive. Love isn't always easy or straightforward or sweet. Can you imagine what it does to a woman to spend over thirty years with a man who can't be satisfied with her alone?"

Eleanore's sculptured face gave way under the pain of her admission, and for a moment she looked her full age. What had Race once told her? Eleanore had her burdens to bear, too. Vicky nodded, for the first time feeling real sympathy for this woman, who had loved Hank, lived with him and never known what it was to be the only woman he cared about. Race's mother had done the intelligent and the brave thing when she'd finally left him; and Race was right—she had married a better man in the end.

"I did love him, Vicky, despite everything. But love can be a means of inflicting pain as well as a means of healing."

"Yes, I know," said Vicky slowly. She remembered herself and Race in the storm, wounding and healing, hurting and comforting.

"Already?"

Vicky nodded pensively.

"Yes. Perhaps you do."

The two women sat in silence for some moments, a strange understanding flowing between them.

"Excuse me, Vicky. I seem to smell something rather peculiar." Eleanore's delicate nose wrinkled in distaste.

"I'm afraid that's me. Sorry," Vicky mumbled in embarrassment.

"What on earth have you been doing?" Eleanore was amused.

"Dipping the walls."

"I beg your pardon."

She explained.

"I see. Race said you worked very hard, and I can see that he wasn't exaggerating."

"What else did he say?"

"I think," Eleanore said diplomatically, "that you had better ask him about that."

"Yes," Vicky agreed in disappointment.

"A remarkable man, wouldn't you say? And he's certainly inherited his father's charm."

"He certainly has," Vicky said dryly.

"As well as his way with words." Eleanore's eyes locked with Vicky's. "I'm still not sure how he managed to talk me into it, but I've decided to withdraw my claim to Oak Hill."

"What?" Vicky's heart leaped.

"Hank wanted you to have it. Race has told me how much this means to you, and . . . frankly this place holds a lot of unhappy memories for me. Once I took possession of it, I would have no use for it whatsoever. So you see—" Eleanore spread her hands in a graceful shrug "—matters really are best left as they are."

"I—I—" Vicky's jaw worked, but she could form no coherent thought.

"My lawyers will draw up the necessary papers next week and forward a copy to you."

"That's why you came here today?" Vicky managed to say at last. "To tell me I can *keep* Oak Hill?"

"Of course."

"Well . . . thank you!" The words seemed inadequate, but they were sincere.

When their business was concluded, the two women realized they had little in common to talk about and agreed to bring the meeting to an end. Vicky did offer to take her on a tour of the kennel, but Eleanore declined, saying she was rather afraid of dogs.

Vicky saw Eleanore to her car and then wandered back into the kennel in a daze. In half an hour her world had been turned right side up. She broke the news to her staff and sent someone to tell Joe Hanley, who was still morosely working with Myron outside.

Suddenly everything seemed to take on new life and purpose. The staff bustled around as excitedly as they had on opening day before Hank's death, cleaning and feeding and arguing. Everything was going to be all right. Vicky was staying for good.

She contemplated the activity with a detached air, a hollow ache still hurting her heart. She knew the cause.

Eleanore said Race had convinced her to let Vicky have the land for the kennel. He clearly could have talked her into letting him have it for his own plans, but he hadn't. He was withdrawing from their bargain and leaving the field clear for Vicky.

So after everything that had happened between them, he had done this for her. And what would he get out of it? Would he come out from California once a year to collect his cut, eventually turning it all over to her? Would he keep searching for a place to build his own dreams?

Vicky looked around at her kennel and the barking boarders almost nostalgically. It wasn't enough anymore. It never would be again.

Race had changed her, had reshaped her needs, and she could never go back to what she had been. She had taught herself, somewhere along the way, that love was an endless, uncritical, sweet-tasting, smooth-flowing, easygoing river and that no person was capable of giving it to her. He had shown her that it was an endless, bottomless river, but it was many other things as well, not all of them easy or sweet.

She had rejected him and his love in a way she had hated other people for rejecting her: because she hadn't wanted to be loved by a dynamic, thinking man but to be adored uncritically and unchangingly. And now that he had let her have it all her own way, would he still want her?

She knew now that he was right: what happened between them was infinitely more important than what happened to her kennel. She couldn't find any more satisfaction in coming home at night to Rebel, who listened without understanding, agreed with everything she said and did, and sought only to please her in exchange for affection and food. She couldn't hold the kennel in her arms at night or awaken with it to laugh and tease in the dawn. Life began in sharing oneself with another person, and everything worthwhile followed.

Would he believe her now? Or would he think she was only rewarding him for falling in with her plans at last? She sighed in exasperation. Wouldn't it be ironic if, now that she finally understood, she couldn't convince him?

She looked around her. There was one way to convince him. It would be the hardest thing she had ever done. It would mean burning her bridges behind her. It would mean giving up the life she knew for one that was going to be very different, and very difficult.

She petted a newly groomed collie as it walked by her, as if saying goodbye to it all in that one caress, and walked out of the building. Her footsteps carried her down the familiar path, past her cottage, over the river to Race's house. His car was there, but he wasn't. He must be around somewhere. She would find him.

Instinct took her to her favorite spot in the shade of an oak tree at the widest part of the river. Race's clothes lay in the shade. She saw him swimming in the river. She went and sat on a rock by the water to watch him, just as he had sat and watched her once.

His strong bronze body sliced through the water, giving her tantalizing glimpses of his naked beauty. His wet hair was dark, showing no hint of his halo. She smiled fondly; he was her angel, halo or not. He seemed to be doing the same thing she had done earlier: trying to chase away his demons with sheer physical exhaustion. But she wanted him to be at least alert enough to talk to her.

"Hey!" she called.

Race went underwater and came up sputtering, flailing and choking.

"Don't you know it's dangerous to swim alone?" she chided him.

"Don't start with me," he warned her.

They watched each other tensely while Race trod water and Vicky sat on her rock.

"Well?" he said at last.

"Eleanore's been and gone. Thank you."

"Don't mention it. Have you got everything you want now?"

"No."

He sighed in exasperation. "What the hell else do you want, Vicky?"

"I want you. I want you to stay with me. Forever."

Race went so still he nearly went underwater again. "Why?"

"Because I love you." It was that simple.

Race snorted cynically. "Is this the pat on the head I get for being loyal, Vicky? Is this the something extra in my food bowl?"

"No. I love you. That's all. I love you the way...the way I think you love me," she said bravely.

"And how is that?" His voice was absolutely flat and expressionless.

"Woman to man. With no reservations. Nothing else matters as much as us," she said steadily.

"Not even your business?" He swam closer to her.

"I don't care about that, Race. Not the way I care about you. You can have the land if you want it. You can build anything you want here. You can bulldoze the kennel and turn it into a tennis court. Just let me love you. Just let me spend fifty years arguing with you and sleeping with you and laughing with you— Race, what are you doing? No, don't! I'll get— Race!"

Vicky shrieked with laughter as he pulled her off her rock and into the river. She bobbed to the surface and gasped for air, only to have it driven from her lungs again as he

wrapped her in a fierce embrace and pressed his lips against
hers. She was dizzy when he pulled away.

"I love you," he whispered. Then he laughed and spun
her around in the water, drenching some passing ducks, who
squawked indignantly.

"I love you!" he repeated. "Crazy and hot tempered and
built like a Greek temple. Oh, Vicky, Vicky, hold me and tell
me again."

She wrapped her arms around his broad shoulders and
did as she was asked, laughing and kissing him.

"Oh, Race, and I thought I'd done all the growing up I
had to do!"

He regarded her five-foot-eleven-inch form and said
warily, "Let's hope there's not much more to go." Then he
frowned. "What's that funny smell?"

"It's me. I was dipping the walls."

"Trying to keep busy?"

"Trying to lock out the pain."

"Me, too."

"There must be a better way than scrubbing walls or
swimming till you drown," she suggested.

"I think I have an idea," Race agreed, and pulled her
sodden T-shirt over her head. He unbuttoned her shorts and
pulled them off, tossing them into the center of the river.

"What am I going to wear later?"

"I'll share," Race assured her.

She swam away from his arms. "I'll race you, Race," she
teased him.

"You'd probably win. Come here," he insisted.

She dog-paddled farther out of his reach. "I'll have to be
the one who teaches our kids to swim. Your sidestroke is
hopeless."

"I've never asked. Do you want children?" he asked seriously.

"Uh-huh. Lots and lots. With golden halos and smoky
eyes and wicked smiles." She let him swim a little closer.

"I'd like a redhead or two," he said, stroking her wet
hair. "In my old age they'll remind me of my great downfall."

"Downfall?"

"I was so sane until I met you. What do you say? If we have half a dozen we won't even need to hire kennel staff anymore."

"What if they want to work on building sites like their father?" she argued.

"Let's have a dozen, then, and we'll each be on the safe side."

"Unless they're misfits and want to do something totally unexpected."

"Victoria! How could *you* possibly produce a misfit?"

She pinched him.

"Ouch! Do that again and we might not have any at all."

"But if we get started now," she said persuasively, "I could have a baby in the spring and be hard at work all winter and summer."

"I don't want you wandering around vicious dogs and slippery hallways while you're pregnant."

"Oh, come on, Race. A woman built like me? I can work all morning, give birth at lunch and be back in time for the closing shift."

"Vicky..." he said uneasily, knowing full well she meant it.

"I guarantee it. No problems. I'm built for hard work. Just feel that." She guided his hand to her strong shoulders. "And for having babies. Just feel that." She guided his hand below the water and sighed as he explored the area in question.

"In that case, shouldn't we get started?" he asked huskily.

"Yes, hurry," she agreed weakly.

Race wrapped his arms around her and pulled her into the shallower water, where he could brace his legs on the river bottom.

All teasing and games forgotten now, Vicky held him and kissed him and loved him as fiercely as her strong body would allow, and he returned her love in kind. He submerged her to chase away the evil smell of flea-and-tick dip, which Vicky had to agree was not a very romantic odor.

Underwater, she teased him and enticed him with her warm mouth until he hauled her roughly back to the surface. She wrapped her legs around his strong, narrow hips and kissed him hungrily as his hand guided hers underwater with unerring accuracy. She felt the shock of the cold river water an instant before his warmth and hardness filled her and completed her.

They moved slowly and naturally together, sweet and unhurried, knowing they could repeat this experience as often as they wanted to for the rest of their lives. The water lapped against their naked bodies as they thrust and heaved, kissed and tasted, touched and caressed, whispered and sighed.

The river of their love swept Vicky along in its whirling current, pulled her into a drowning whirlpool of giddy delight and rapturous pleasure and flung her down a towering, rushing, roaring waterfall of satisfaction to float at last, buoyant and free, in its sweet calm. And she knew Race had gone on the journey with her, was its source, was its center, was her companion and partner in the overwhelming beauty of that torrential pleasure.

He carried her out of the water when it was over and lay with her on the soft grass in the shade of the oak tree, veiled from prying eyes by its heavy, leafy, low-hanging branches.

Their eyes held with warm, happy love. Vicky ran her fingers through his damp hair and touched his face lightly. He pressed a tender kiss into her palm, and they whispered words of love and pleased satisfaction.

"It won't always be green grass and sweet kisses, Vicky," he warned her later as they lay together in the lazy afternoon. "I won't always be adoring and uncritical."

"You almost never are."

"I mean—"

"I know what you mean. You mean you'll love me like a man and not a pet."

He nodded and regarded her warily, not sure she was ready for that yet.

She smiled calmly at him. "I've made my choice, and I can handle it. I'm strong enough for anything now. What I get from you is worth learning to adjust to . . . normal life."

He kissed her.

"I meant what I said before, Race. You still win our original agreement. I'd be going out of business if you hadn't fixed things for me. The land's yours if you want it."

"You really mean that, don't you?"

"I still won't like it, but I'd rather have you."

He drew in a breath and closed his eyes. "That's all I've ever wanted, Vicky. Just to matter most to you. I just wanted you to love me the way I love you."

"I do." She snuggled up to him.

"Anyhow, I guess I decided a long time ago to let you keep it."

"But didn't you tell your secretary you thought you had reason to stay?"

"I meant you, you idiot. I was already hopelessly . . . irrational and out of control where you were concerned. That was how Wade put it, anyhow. I just wanted to live with you." He added smugly, "I knew I could make you see it my way in the end."

"You arrogant bas— Sorry."

"I've never denied it," he teased her.

"So you *don't* want me to close down?"

"No. I couldn't do that to you. I love you. Anyhow, we have too much fun over there."

"Fun!" she repeated. "I work twelve hours a day in the steaming heat, cleaning, scrubbing, feeding, slogging heavy—"

"Well, it's fun for me, anyhow. I only show up when something exciting is happening: mad dogs on the loose, irate fathers with double-barreled shotguns, water fights, mass hysteria. . . . My past looks positively dull in comparison to this summer."

"I see your point," said Vicky dryly. "But even with our bargain . . . solved, money will be tight for a year or two," she warned him.

"I couldn't take all that away from you, even if we were going broke," he said gallantly.

"Why didn't you tell me, you idiot? We wouldn't have been at each other's throats all this time!"

"A lot of reasons. If I told you, you'd expect me to leave the way we had agreed, and I wanted to stay. Mostly I thought I'd never be sure if you loved me because you loved me or because I'd been obedient and cooperative. And because I wanted you to decide for yourself what you wanted most. I thought you *had* decided that night in my bedroom—Vicky, that was the most incredible night of my life. How can you say you don't know anything about men? But then you really shook me up the next day."

"Oh, Race—"

"That next night, right here, I thought it was all over for good after what you said. I thought I'd been an idiot to think I could ever make you want me more than you wanted a building full of two hundred yapping dogs. To have that as a rival is pretty deflating to a man's ego!"

She had to laugh. "But at least you know who won hands down," she pointed out. "But what about those building plans I saw? What about the inquiries you've been making in town?"

"Well, that stretch of land on the eastern boundary is so far away from the kennel you can't even see or hear the kennel from there. Or this spot—I checked. I don't want anyone else watching you swimming in the mornings. We don't use that land, Vicky, so I can build something I really want to there and sell it off. Then I'll have something solid to show people here, to get others interested in my work."

"You don't want to go back to California?"

He shook his head decisively. "No, this is home now. And you're here." He added wickedly, "Besides, I expect you to get rich enough to support me in style, and then I really won't ever have to build another thing I don't want to."

"Will you build us a house?"

"Someday. But for now why don't we live in the manor house? I'm working wonders in there. I'm a genius," he said modestly.

"I will *not* live in that house until you do something about the kitchen and the bathrooms. You can live with me until you do."

"Fair enough. And after we move, maybe Wade will want to live in the cottage."

"Wade? Is he willing to leave California?"

"He might be, if we provide him with enough grandchildren. Anyhow, he'll certainly come to visit to keep you and me from tearing each other apart."

"I rather enjoy tearing you apart, Race." She touched him teasingly. He drew in a sharp breath, but his eyes were serious when he spoke.

"Did you enjoy it the night of the storm?"

Vicky, too, was serious as she answered. "You know I did."

"You looked so haunted after that."

"You...showed me something in myself I'd never known was there. I was spooked."

He kissed her softly. "So was I. I was crazy with jealousy and wanting you. You set off something in me that I couldn't control."

"This, maybe?" She kissed him as hungrily and almost as violently as she had on that night. He responded instantly. They were both breathing heavily when they pulled apart. "It's still there," she said. "Something besides jealousy and wanting. Something deeper and stronger and darker than that. It's the way we love." She nestled contentedly against him and they touched each other with exquisite tenderness, marveling at the depth and range of their feelings for each other.

After a long while Vicky said, "I wonder if Hank set us all up for this. Do you think he always knew?"

"I doubt it. Things just had a way of turning to gold for him. Only this time he's not around for the payoff. You and I are." He kissed her.

"But how on earth did you convince Eleanore?"

"Let's just say I told her the truth but I expressed it in a way she could appreciate."

"I see," said Vicky cynically. "And it had nothing to do with charm and sweet talk?"

"Well, maybe a little. Actually I kind of like her. I'm glad as all hell she wasn't my mom, though. I guess everything really did happen for the best."

"I kind of like her, too. And she was sure taken with you, you remarkable young man, you."

"Ah, so she noticed."

"Race, I think I'm very impressed with myself for having ever hurt your ego or undermined your self-confidence."

"Blowing people out of the water seems to come naturally to you," he pointed out nastily. "By the way, you might say a kind word or two to Désirée. She thinks you're never going to forgive her—"

"Oh, that dummy. Oh, all right. I'll say something nice. I can afford to be generous now. Poor kid. It was a rough way to discover the opposite sex."

"Speaking of discovering the opposite sex..." Race's hands wandered over her inquisitively and possessively.

"Before you make another move, I feel I should point something out."

"What's that?" His strong hand kneaded the muscles of her back.

"Unless you want another bastard to be born at Oak Hill, shouldn't you ask me to marry you?"

"Now what, Victoria, would I get out of marrying you?" he teased her. "Besides endless aggravation, I mean. Since I already own half of everything you've got, what can you offer me?"

"Lots!" she insisted. "I own a dozen pairs of shorts."

"Each more threadbare than the last," Race said critically.

"And two dozen T-shirts."

"Each skimpier than the last," Race said appreciatively.

"Actually not *quite* two dozen, since one of them is floating around in the river now."

"Sorry. What else?"

"I have a whole bookcase full of books on dog care."

"Not interested."

"And a dog."

"Who's almost as crazy and unpredictable as you are. What else?"

"I think that's all," said Vicky disappointedly. "Nothing entices you?"

"I wouldn't say that exactly." His hands found her breasts. She sighed longingly. "What the hell, I can afford to be generous now. Vicky, will you marry me?"

"I'll have to think about it."

Race looked at her in astonishment.

"Isn't that what a girl's supposed to say?" she teased him.

"You picked a hell of a moment to start saying the right thing."

She kissed him. "Yes. Let's get married. In the fall. I have too much work to do now to be bothered with a wedding."

"How romantic you are," Race said dryly.

"I'm romantic when it counts," she insisted. She tried to prove her point.

"Yes, you are," Race agreed weakly a few moments later.

They were silent then, except for longing sighs and murmured endearments. The world seemed made only for the two of them....

"Rebel! Rebel! Come back here, dammit!" Brian shouted.

There was some happy barking, followed by deep, heavy whoofing.

"Myron, no! Joe, can't you teach that dog anything?"

Vicky and Race rolled apart in astonishment as Rebel went tearing past them and jumped into the river. Myron followed close behind, making such a huge splash some of the water hit Vicky and Race.

"What the hell is going on?" she gasped, sitting up.

Race covered his eyes with one arm and didn't answer.

"Rebel! I'm gonna skin you alive!" Brian's voice was very near now.

"Brian!" she shouted from the shadows of the oak tree. "Stay right where you are! Don't come any closer!"

"Vicky? What—"

"That's an order!" said Race.

There was a stunned silence. Then Brian said, "Ohh," in a disgustingly smug, knowing voice. "So you two finally made up, did you?"

"Never mind that!" she snapped. "What's going on?"

Rebel and Myron were creating total havoc in the river, and the noise level had exceeded a dull roar.

"Rebel grabbed a tractor part and ran off. Myron took off after her. I think Joe's gonna need a chiropractor."

"What tractor part? Not the one I just paid a blue fortune for!" Vicky demanded.

"Yes."

"Well, don't just stand there! Go get my dog!"

"Vicky..." Race said significantly.

"And—and keep your eyes closed!"

"What?" said Brian.

"Just do as you're told!" she insisted.

Brian ran past them, eyes closed, and fell headfirst into the river. He bobbed to the surface, sputtering, flailing and choking. Vicky tried to go after him. Race restrained her.

"Put some clothes on first," he insisted.

She drew on his shirt, buttoned it quickly and ran out to the river's edge, leaving Race pulling on his trousers in the shadows. The shirt came to midthigh, but Brian's eyes bulged nonetheless when he saw her. There was something wet and limp sitting on his head. He pulled it off and looked at it. It was Vicky's T-shirt. Brian looked at her with wicked delight.

"Lose something, Vic?" he asked meaningfully.

"Give me that!"

"Couldn't be yours, could it? How do you suppose it got here?"

"Brian, if I have to replace that tractor part, I'll take it out of your hide!"

Myron swam over and gleefully pounced on Brian. Rebel swam farther out to the center of the river, trying to catch up with some angry ducks. Myron seemed to be having some success in his efforts to drown Brian.

"Race!" Vicky shouted. "Go get Rebel! Get that part away from her!" She added grimly, rolling up her sleeves, "And I am going to make sure Myron doesn't rob me of the pleasure of strangling Brian with my bare hands!"

She leaped into the water and tried to break up the two thrashing bodies as they alternately barked and shouted.

"Oh, well," sighed Race. "I might as well get used to it. This is the way it'll be for the next fifty years or so."

He leaped into the river after the rest of them, and life carried on as usual at Oak Hill.

* * * * *

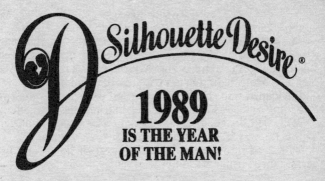

1989
IS THE YEAR
OF THE MAN!

What makes a romance? A special man, of course, and Silhouette Desire celebrates that fact with *twelve* of them! From Mr. January to Mr. December, every month has a tribute to the Silhouette Desire hero—our **MAN OF THE MONTH!**

Sexy, macho, charming, irritating . . . irresistible! Nothing can stop these men from sweeping you away. Created by some of your favorite authors, each man is custom-made for pleasure—*reading* pleasure—so don't miss a single one.

Mr. January is Blake Donavan in RELUCTANT FATHER by Diana Palmer
Mr. February is Hank Branson in THE GENTLEMAN INSISTS by Joan Hohl
Mr. March is Carson Tanner in NIGHT OF THE HUNTER by Jennifer Greene
Mr. April is Slater McCall in A DANGEROUS KIND OF MAN by Naomi Horton
Mr. May is Luke Harmon in VENGEANCE IS MINE by Lucy Gordon
Mr. June is Quinn McNamara in IRRESISTIBLE by Annette Broadrick

And that's only the half of it—
so get out there and find your man!

Silhouette Desire's

MAN OF THE MONTH . . .

ATTRACTIVE, SPACE SAVING BOOK RACK

Display your most prized novels on this handsome and sturdy book rack. The hand-rubbed walnut finish will blend into your library decor with quiet elegance, providing a practical organizer for your favorite hard-or soft-covered books.

Only $9.95

Approximately 16" x 8" when assembled

Assembles in seconds!

To order, rush your name, address and zip code, along with a check or money order for $10.70* ($9.95 plus 75¢ postage and handling) payable to *Silhouette Books*.

Silhouette Books
Book Rack Offer
901 Fuhrmann Blvd.
P.O. Box 1396
Buffalo, NY 14269-1396

Offer not available in Canada.

*New York and Iowa residents add appropriate sales tax.

BKR-2A

 Silhouette Desire ®

COMING
NEXT MONTH

#481 NIGHT OF THE HUNTER—Jennifer Greene
Meet our March *Man of the Month*, Carson Tanner. Proud.
Elusive. He prized freedom above all else, but when he met
Charly Erickson, freedom never seemed lonelier.

#482 CHANCES ARE—Erica Spindler
Men were a challenge to unconventional Veronique Delacroix.
But when she decided to date her boss on a dare, she found the
stakes getting too high—even for her!

#483 THE ROOKIE PRINCESS—Janice Kaiser
Coach Nick Bartlett couldn't believe a woman the press had
dubbed the ''Rookie Princess'' was now his boss. But Hillary
James was nothing like he'd expected . . . and all he'd dreamed of.

#484 AS GOOD AS GOLD—Cathie Linz
From the moment smooth-talking attorney Bryce Stephenson
strode into her life accusing her of gold-digging, Susan Cantrell
sensed trouble. And Bryce was trouble—in more ways than one.

#485 WOMAN IN THE SHADOWS—Sara Chance
He appeared in *Southern Comfort*—now James Southerland is
back in a story of his own with Suzanne Frazier, an intriguing
woman playing a dangerous game of deception.

#486 BUTTERFLY—Jo Ann Algermissen
Handsome ex-rebel Seth Kimble returned home only to find
Vanessa Monarch caught in a gilded net. Only he could free her
and let her fly . . . straight into his arms.

AVAILABLE NOW:

#475 THE GENTLEMAN INSISTS
Joan Hohl

**#476 A MAN AROUND THE
HOUSE**
Donna Carlisle

#477 A PIRATE AT HEART
Marcy Gray

#478 ONE SULTRY SUMMER
Laura Leone

#479 HIGH JINX
Nancy Gramm

#480 ONLY FOREVER
Linda Lael Miller